Like
Clockwork

H.J. Stamm

ISBN-13: 978-1-9990883-0-9

For Anoop, Kaylee, Laurie, Lloyd, Mari-Louise, Paul, Pearl, Sukhi, Suzannah, and the Torfam. Thank you for believing in me, even when I didn't believe in myself.

"I am wiser than this man; for neither of us knows anything, but this man thinks he knows something when he does not, whereas I, as I do not know anything, do not think I do. I seem, then, in just this little thing, to be wiser than this man, that what I do not know I do not think I know."

-Socrates

CHAPTER 1
WELCOME TO VANCOUVER

Pigeon lay in bed, fully clothed. A light drizzle played against the window in a soothing staccato. Maria lay next to her, fingertips playing through her matted braids. Every time she touched one of the charms tied into her hair, Pigeon would tell the story of how she had acquired it. They had played this game before, but they both enjoyed it just the same.

"What's this one?" asked Maria, touching a spent cartridge. "Is it new?'

"I had to take a pot shot at a dealer the other day," answered Pigeon. "No one died, and I got paid." Maria nodded appreciatively.

"And this one?" she asked, fingering a

small gold ring.

"The only thing my parents left with me when they abandoned me. I swiped it back during my first Run."

Her first Run. The Children's Employment and Education Centre, or CHEEK for short. She flitted through the System like a shadow. Running was in her blood.

"The first Run is always the hardest," reminisced Pigeon. "The first steps are in your mind. The knowledge that, once you start, you can never stop. That every breath you will take will be on borrowed time. That the System will hunt you down. That it always does, in the end."

Some people never chose to Run. The System called them Citizens. To people like Pigeon, they were Squatters: passive, untrustworthy, living off crumbs. Maria fell somewhere in the middle, not a Runner herself but plugged into the underworld enough that she was not a straight Squatter.

Pigeon suspected that Maria viewed her life with a certain amount of romanticism, like some sort of swashbuckling action hero. The truth was that there was no romanticism to

Pigeon's life. The light had gone out long ago, and she had to harden her heart to survive.

Running in Vancouver was like pushing a dull blade against your forearm: a little painful, but unlikely to leave any permanent marks.

"What's the scan?" asked Maria, taking a long drag of a cigarette.

"You have the time?" asked Pigeon.

"It's about... this time," said Maria, flashing the bioluminescent display embedded in the flesh of her left forearm.

"Edgy. Time for me to tab in," said Pigeon, getting out of bed and grabbing the paper bag full of stolen hard drives she had left on the small kitchen table. She needed to be downtown to meet her fence, and she knew the commute would be miserable in the rain. Popping her collar against the cold, she set out.

****

"Freedom"

The word loomed over her, carved from pink light. She stopped briefly, the billboard casting an uneven shadow across her pockmarked face. The hologram shifted; it was an advertisement for a trendy new designer narcotic. She kept walking. She had no interest in that sort of freedom. It was a trap, one she'd seen others fall into it. The feeling of being numb, warm, content. Feelings designed to make you stand still. To make it easier for the System to catch up to you. She knew a lot of Runners, too many, who'd been caught that way. She wondered if they had done it intentionally, if they had felt the System closing in and chosen to let themselves be taken while their minds floated on a bed of clouds.

She put the thought out of her head as she pushed open the door to the restaurant. It was a Squatter place, something ritzy and middle class. It smelled like bleach and alcohol, a combination she hated. Too clean. Too respectable. Everyone was wearing dark and drab colours, a lot of black and beige. Pigeon, in her layers of tattered and dirty street clothes, stuck out like a sore thumb. A bald man in the corner booth spotted her over his shoulder and signaled at her with an open palm. She made her way over to him, weaving through tables. She was on edge already, but her Runner's Sense told her to be extra cautious: it appeared as though he had invited someone to sit in on their deal.

"Hey," he said flatly. As Pigeon slid into the seat next to him. Pigeon had been dealing with this same miserable fence for almost two weeks, and she took this greeting as something bordering on sentimental.

"It's all here," she said, resting a paper bag on the table in front of them.

"Can I see them," he said, sliding his hand into the bag and producing a slim plastic rectangle. He tilted it over, looking for imperfections.

"500 exabytes," said Pigeon. "Like you wanted." The man grunted, as if unhappy that he would be expected to pay the agreed upon price. He started to reach into his pocket, then hesitated. Pigeon noticed this, but kept her face flat.

"You know," he growled. ""I've got a friend you should meet..." Her Runner's Sense traced a cold shiver up her neck, while her hand drifted down to her waist.

"Why waste words when there's money to be made," replied Pigeon, throwing his words back at him. He grunted, sensing the irony.

The large man across from her shifted.

In one smooth motion she produced a bulky tube from her hip, pressed the tip of the tube to his forehead, pulled the trigger. There was a click, like a very loud stapler, and the big man slumped over, blood starting to bead from the nickel sized hole between his eyes. She turned just as quickly to face her now-former associate. He was fumbling with something tucked into his suit jacket, and she took the opportunity to cock the pistol and press the barrel to the underside of his chin. Another sharp click, and he slumped face down into his plate of calamari.

Pigeon quickly scanned the room. No one had heard the subsonic rounds over the din of the music and shattered conversations. Good. Two seemingly unconscious men would attract a lot of attention, and eventually someone would notice the blood. Then all hell would break loose. In a Runner bar it wouldn't have been a problem. But Pigeon knew she couldn't trust Squatters to mind their own business.

Hoping to salvage some profit from this

miserable transaction, she slipped a deft hand into her ex-fence's pocket. She immediately felt a large wad of plastic currency, and was just about to withdraw her prize when her fingertips brushed against something smooth and round. A key ring maybe? She hooked a finger around it and stuffed the whole handful into her pocket without looking. Stuffing the bag of solid states into her pocket, Pigeon slipped out into the night, her mind racing. She needed to Run, that much was clear. But part of being a good Runner was knowing how to balance haste with sense.

After only a moment's hesitation, she had decided on a plan, one of many that constantly swirled through her mind, being revised and re-revised with every waking moment: a quick trip to the squalid basement that she called home to grab a few things, then she would disappear. The light drizzle was building into a steady rain. Pigeon flipped her hood up and quickened her pace, head down, making a beeline for the nearest SkyTrain station.

Pigeon swiped the microchip embedded in her palm over the flat surface of the digital turnstile. The screen gave a sharp beep, and briefly flashed a picture of someone who bore a passing resemblance to her; could even have been her, if she was five years younger and white.

The chip was a mod, designed to let her pass through the System without being a part of it. The identity manifest had been purchased off the dark web, and the uploading process was no more than a sharp pinprick on the back of her hand, a quick trip to a back alley salon. She could have paid more for a perfect replica of herself, scrubbed clean to avoid suspicion. But she also knew that some of the cheaper mods would flash info so unconvincing she didn't know why people bothered chipping up at all. She supposed, as with all Runners, that it was some calculation of haste over sense. As far as Pigeon was concerned, it was always better to keep your wits and move quickly, than to break away from the pack completely and risk singling yourself out.

She made her way across the platform and ducked onto the train just as the doors slid shut. Three short tones, and the train rocketed into a pitch black tunnel. Pigeon slumped down on the chipped vinyl bench seat, her reflection glowering back at her from the bank of windows opposite. Strips of advertising lit the train with a gloomy, dim light. She cast a quick glance around the carriage, taking stock of her surroundings.

A couple of mohawked young women with matching safety pins pushed through the bridges of their noses were breathless fingering each other through stud encrusted leather pants. An older model 'droid sat in the corner, tattered synthskin hanging in ribbons from an emaciated frame. It was watching them fervently from the corner of it's one good eye, the aged servos in its exposed arm twitched in a rhythmic spasm. No one so much as glanced in Pigeon's direction, and she allowed herself the luxury of relaxing momentarily.

A brief flash of electric pink and blue as the train rocketed out into the night, rooftop holos flickering and shimmering. Rain clouds stretched across the sky like gritty grey octopus, tentacles clinging to the mountains that surrounded the city, slimy bodies twinning through the downtown high-rises. Large raindrops slanted to the ground, driven by a cold sea breeze. In the distance, the jagged teeth of high-rise urban sprawl tore at the dirty horizon. Sodium street lights cast bleached their surroundings an unearthly pallor, islands in a shifting sea of headlights and traffic signals.

Glittering jewels, endlessly receding.

Heavy raindrops hammered the scarred Plexiglas windows with the sound of a pot of water boiling on a stove. A second set of three tones, and a cool female voice with a slight metallic twinge called out the name of the station as the train ground to a halting stop. Pigeon used the momentum of the train to catapult herself out of her seat and through the doors just as they were beginning to dilate open. Her dirty canvas low-tops dancing lightly over the filthy station floor, she made her way up the stairs two at a time. She had just barely reached the top step a little out of breathe when a baby-faced man with stringy, dirty blonde hair and an orange down-filled vest over a greasy jean jacket shoved his way past her. She stumbled, but just barely managed to catch herself.

"Asshole," Pigeon muttered quietly, regaining her footing and falling back into her stride. Rounding the corner, she found herself at the tail end of a queue. Peeking over the shoulders of the people in front of her, she saw that it was a fare check. There were three meathead transit cops standing in a delta formation, decked out in matching black PASGT uniforms and balaclavas. One officer was holding a device that looked like a hair dryer plugged into to an attaché case, except that where the locks would normally have been there were instead a set of three small lightbulbs.

He was running the handset over the palms of people in line, and letting them pass after ensuring that the light was flashing green. The other two cops stood behind him to either side with their hands resting on their sidearms, open-bolt machine-pistols that fired caseless sabots in a three-round burst. As the line of people slowly made their way through the check point, Pigeon took notice of the asshole a few positions ahead of her in the line. He kept running the flat of his hand over his vest pockets in a nervous, repetitive action. Thick droplets of sweat beaded his forehead. Pigeon knew how this little drama would play out. She had seen it a hundred times, and each time she did, she took a little lesson for herself.

This was a Runner, about to be ensnared by the System.

The scruffy young man stepped up to the transit cop in turn. Wincing in anticipation, he held out his palm. Pigeon noticed that his hand was visibly trembling. As if on cue, the fare reader flashed red and let out a low tone. One of the transit cops stepped into action, breaking formation as he extended his riot baton. The polymer cylinder gave an electronic hum as he pulled his arm back and drove the tip into the Runner's stomach. There was a loud crack like a clap of thunder, and the young man was double over in pain, convulsing slightly as his lips uttered an unearthly shriek of pain. The transit cop gave another two quick blows to his abdomen, forcing him to the ground and driving him up against the wall.

"Runner!" shouted the transit cop over the shrieks and cracks of the continued assault. "You are under arrest for breach of peace! Stop resisting!"

With lackadaisical indifference, the transit cop with the fare reader went back to checking palms, his compatriot looking on with the boredom that came only through well-worn routine.

Pigeon kept an eye on them with her peripheral vision while she passed through the checkpoint unmolested. She silently thanked her god that she had done so; stepping onto the dirty, rain splattered street, she was only a few blocks from her home, and only a few more than that from a successful Run. As usual, her calculation of haste over sense had paid off

Pigeon knew what had to be done. She spent every moment that she wasn't Running planning the next. She had imagined every detail, poured over it in her mind. Keep the Run going, keep the momentum going, always forward, always moving. She knew that there were two components to a successful Run: stay alive, and face no consequences. Travel light, check you baggage at the door. Never look back. Always forward. It kept it her up most nights, constant hypervigilance taking its toll on her, visible in her silver hairs, her awful complexion, and the rings of dark flesh underneath her eyes.

Around the back, down a flight of stairs, turn a corner and down a second flight and she was home. She missed stepping over the pool of standing rainwater in front of the door and grimaced as she felt her shoes fill with water. Shouldering open the door, she immediately began tossing her belongings into the stained rucksack she kept hanging near the door. When she thought she had all of the essentials slung over her back, Pigeon gave the abode a quick once over, finishing by patting herself down.

There was a bulge in her pocket that surprised her, until she remembered the reason she was Running in the first place: double-crossed by that miserable old flat. Digging around with her short, stubby fingers, she produced a large of wad of polymer bills, and a small model scorpion made from twisted copper wiring. When she was pilfering the body of her former fence, she must have mistaken the curve of the hooked tail for the loop of a key ring.

That was the least impressive of her haul, however; riffling through the wad of cash, she had almost two-thousand dollars in small bills, unmarked except for the single crease running through the centre. Between that and the street value of the stolen hard-drives packed in her bag, she had enough money to allow herself to disappear for a respectable amount of time, completely off the grid. Edgy. After tonight, she would need to tab out for a while, at least until the heat came off.

"Pigeon!" said a voice from somewhere behind her, causing her to start. "Hey slowpoke. Hurry up. What are you doing? Hurry up." She whipped around; there was no one in the suite with her.

"Shit," she said aloud. Now was not a good time. Had it been a month since her last injection? Maybe more. Like most Runners, Pigeon had trouble keeping track of time. "Meds. Add it to the list."

A sudden pounding at the the door. "VPD! Open up!" Pigs. She didn't know how, but they had found her almost immediately. She paid her monthly rent in cash, signed digitally using her modded chip. How? How did they trace her here? She put the thought out of her head, the only thing on her mind needed to be the Run. She wormed her way through the bathroom window, kicking it shut behind her.

Clambering to her feet, she set out at a brusque walk, melting into a passing crowd of people waiting for the light to change. If she could only make it a few more blocks she could be back on the SkyTrain, and this Run would be more than half complete. Lost in thought, she had barely made it more than few steps when a deep, masculine voiced called her name from somewhere behind her. She turned, instinctively-

And was met with a sudden blinding pain in the centre of her face, dropping her to her knees and filling her mouth with blood; her nose had been broken.

"Pigeon Smith!" shouted the same deep voice. "You are under arrest for fifteen counts of breach of peace!" There was pressure between her shoulder blades, forcing her down onto her stomach, grinding her cheek into the gritty, stinking sidewalk.

Stupid, stupid, stupid, she thought, as her arms were torqued behind her and she felt the polymer flexicuffs coil and tighten around her wrists. How could she be so stupid? She was an expert runner; how had she let herself get caught so easily?

As she was shoved into the back of the cruiser, blood still pouring over her face and draining down the back of her throat, a thought occurred to her: she had been set-up. More than likely, she had been followed from as far back as the restaurant. With the realisation, she slumped down in her seat, dejected. She didn't know what would be next, but whatever it was she was sure that it wouldn't be good.

CHAPTER 2
OUT OF THE FRYING PAN

The holding cell was cold, cinderblocks painted white, lit with harsh fluorescent lights that stung Pigeon's eyes and reminded her uncomfortably of the CHEEK. She held her hand in her hands, willing tears to come that she knew never would, running her fingers over her newly shaved head. The first thing they had done when they brought her in was shake her down, before shearing the hair off her head.

All of her trinkets, memories twinned into her hair, had been dumped unceremoniously in the incinerator. They had destroyed her identity, turning her into just another number; for a Runner, the ultimate signal of defeat. Her parents had been in that hair, her first Run, Anita…

Jesus, thought Pigeon. What would Anita think of this situation? What would she say? She always knew exactly what to say.

****

"Remember baby, the sun will always come out." Anita pulled back an ear-lobe to reveal the small tattoo on her upper neck. "It always does. Eventually." Pigeon was laying on top of her, her bony frame and soft coolness pressing into her chest.

They were both fully clothed, but the tenderness of the moment filled them with a different kind of warmth. They lay there, in a tiny cot, wrapped up in the sheets for what felt like hours, bodies twinned together like threads of a rope, the feeble air conditioning unit running

"Threads of a noose," said a small voice in the dark. Pigeon ignored it, pressing her face deeper into Anita's dirty hair. When she was with Anita, she felt like nothing could touch her. Like she was invincible.

Her nose had finally stopped bleeding, coagulated blood crusting her lips and chin. Someone had slapped a piece of medical tape across the bridge of her nose to hold it in place. Listening to some of the cops talk amongst themselves, she gathered that she had taken the butt of an assault rifle to the face. Now, facing the prospect of an eternity in custody, Pigeon thought that she would be better off dead. Better to die free than to live a long, ruined life in the maw of the System.

Pigeon's contemplation of her inevitable early demise was interrupted by the heavy door swinging open, and then thundering shut as an overweight, balding man in a short sleeve dress shirt and burgundy tie dropped into the seat across from her. Pigeon noticed a stained spot on his tie, about halfway down. It looked like marinara.

"Hullo, Pigeon," he said in a bored growl, "My name is Detective Pendleton." Pigeon managed a grimace in response, and he continued speaking without looking her in the eye. "I have better things to do than to frag around with street-rat Runners, so I'm gonna make this quick and to the point." Pigeon sat up a little straighter in her seat. This was not what she was expecting.

Pendleton continued, "You did me a solid, clipping that old bastard when you did. So I'm gonna make you a deal, a life for a life. All that cash you had on you? That goes into my retirement fund. Same goes for your pistol, and those hot solid-states. Your chip is gonna get wiped, and we're gonna dump you out on the street with a twenty-four hour head start. What do you think?"

Pendleton looked up suddenly, examining Pigeon's face as if he had just realised that they were in the same room. There was a hunger in those baby blue eyes. A hunger that Pigeon recognised, and despised. A hunger that told her she was lucky that Pendleton was not making a deal that exacted a heavier toll. It was a bum deal, totally one sided, and they both knew it. She mulled it over in mind for a few seconds, but she already knew what the answer would be. "Okay," said Pigeon finally. What choice did she really have? Pendleton grunted in approval and produced what appeared to be a thick ceramic drink-coaster.

"Place your hand here," he said, with an air of routine.

Pigeon obeyed, and Pendleton

depressed a small plastic tab on the side of the device. There was a whir, and then a white hot flash of pain seared its way through Pigeon's palm and travelled up her arm where it settled in her shoulder as a dull ache. She swore involuntarily, rotating her shoulder in a vain attempt to assuage the pain. Grumbling to herself, Pigeon allowed herself to be escorted out of the room by Pendleton, his hand lingering uncomfortably on the small of her back.

She was halfway out the door when Pendleton called her back. "Hey!" he said. "Don't forget your personal effects."

"Personal effects?" repeated Pigeon flatly. What personal effects? They had taken all of her personal effects. Pendleton produced the wire scorpion and pushed it into her hands.

"That's a cool little toy you've got. Good luck out there, kid," said Pendleton.

Stepping out onto the street, Pigeon felt a lump forming in her throat. Rain splattered onto her bald head, streaming over her face. It felt like tears, the one thing she wanted right now but couldn't have. Didn't have, not since Anita had left her. Screwing up her eyes, Pigeon arched her arm back, about to throw the model away in frustration, when she felt the weight shift unexpectedly. Drawing it close to her face, she gave it a little shake and heard a light rattling. Was there something inside of it?

Nunya's diner was a few blocks away from the police station. Moving quickly to the back, she slipped into the washroom and scrubbed the dry blood off her face and turning her sweater inside out to cover the stains. Coming out of the washroom, she eyed to room and spotted an empty seat with a half-drunk coffee and a mouthful of sandwich on a plate. Sliding into the booth, Pigeon stuffed the food into her mouth and the tip into her pocket. She swirled the coffee mug, trying her best to seem like she belonged.

Placing the metal scorpion on the Formica table top, she pushed it around with her fingertips for a few moments while a waitress drifted over and refilled her coffee from a carbon-fibre carafe. Sipping at her piping hot beverage, she rolled the figurine over in the palm of her hand. The filament was intricate, hand woven from a single strand of copper, folded over and into itself. Someone had put a lot of time into this single, ornate trinket.

Pigeon pushed the tail flat with the palm of her hand and twirled it counter-clockwise, the complicated weave unravelling easily. She peeled the claws apart, and the whole sculpture came undone in her hands, a small chunk of plastic tumbling onto the table with a clatter. She picked the thing up and twirled it between her fingertips. It appeared to be some sort of digital storage, but she had never seen anything quite like it.

Slipping the copper coil and its contents into her pocket, she fed the quarters from the stolen tip into the payphone just outside the diner. She dialed the number that she had committed to memory, casting a quick glance over her shoulder.

"You're stupid," said a voice beside her. "You're worthless. You're gonna get caught."

"Hey," said Pigeon into the receiver. "It's me. I got picked up by the System. They took my cash and burned my mod."

"Shit. I'm lucky to be hearing your voice," said Maria.

"Tell me about it," replied Pigeon.

"You need work?" responded Maria.

"You're stupid and worthless. You got caught once. It's gonna happen again," said the voice.

"Yes," said Pigeon.

"I know a guy, my uncle" replied Maria. "He'll know someone with work."

****

Street lights reflected against the black sky and wet asphalt, desaturating the night and bleaching it a sickly, chemical orange. The storm had passed, but not before staining the ground with a cold, glassy sheen. The sounds of the city echoed across the night: the grinding of the dockyards, the elevated SkyTrain clattering along the track, the cyclical hum of a power transformer, wailing sirens, car alarms, a distant jet plane. This was Surrey, across the river, Vancouver's ugly step-sister.

Pigeon's shoes fell with wet, empty slaps against the dirty sidewalk, her breath hanging in the damp air. She had been walking these streets for hours, head down, hands balled into fists in her coat pockets, scanning the cars parked against the curb with her peripheral vision.

She was looking for an early model sedan, foreign made and neutral toned. A quick glance over her shoulder to make sure she wasn't being followed; her eyes flitted along the roof tops, checking for silhouettes. When she finally what she had been looking for, she breathed a small sigh of relief: she wasn't paid by the hour, and she had already been out here for far too long. As she approached the passenger side door, two voices started whispering to each other:

"What's she doing?"

"She's committing a crime."

"She's a criminal."

"She's a bad person."

"She's going to get caught."

"She deserves to be caught."

Pigeon ignored them, fishing out a small ring of rough-cut brass keys from inside her coat. She inserted the first bump key into the lock, jiggling it roughly while applying light pressure. After a few moments without results she tried the second, and then the third. It wasn't until the fourth attempt that she heard the tell-tale thunk of the car door unlocking.

"She did it."

"I didn't think she could."

She slid into the driver's seat, swearing as she passed gracelessly over the centre console. One of the voices snickered.

"Shut up," Pigeon growled to herself, inserting into the ignition switch the same key that she had used to open the door. The engine turned over and she dropped the handbrake, pulling away from the curb. She rolled down the driver's side window and turned up the heat, letting the cold night roll across her face as she turned onto King George Boulevard. The whispers were still there, but she could no longer make out what they were saying, distinction lost in the rush of moving air.

At the intersection of King George and 104th she had to stop at a red-light, pulling up next to a white-and-royal blue RCMP cruiser. She could feel her heart pounding in her chest, and a tightness in her throat. Luckily for her, the officer was distracted by a group of four or five teenagers in oversized down jackets standing on the street corner. They were passing a bottle in a brown paper bag between them, laughing and shouting expletives at one another. The light turned green and the police officer peeled off, letting her continue on her way. As she neared the water, the acrid scent of chemically treated wood filled her lungs, the mills that skirted the shoreline venting their waste. Lime green rectangles flitted by overhead, signage for Downtown, and the boroughs of Burnaby, Port Coquitlam, and New Westminster.

Her destination was the latter: steep hills and claustrophobic quays, brick tenements and highways cantilevered over narrow one-way streets, packed with neon lit dive-bars. She accelerated, pretending to race the SkyTrain that ran parallel to the Patullo Bridge. The train never slept; neither did the city and neither did she. On the Vancouver side of the Fraser River, the trains veered off to the left, sinking underneath the ground. Pigeon had the sudden, unsettling vision of a fat worm, burrowing into a sandy beach. She turned in the opposite direction, navigating a series of looping switchbacks that eventually brought her down to within a few blocks of the waterfront.

Maria had set her up with a guy named Gerry, a local who operated a chop shop out of his brother's legitimate dealership. Maria said he was always willing to pay cash for cars, no questions asked.

"Luckily," she muttered to herself, "I can get cars and need the cash."

Turning into the car lot, she drove around back and parked in an empty space beside one of the service bays. Killing the engine and retrieving her ring of skeleton keys, she got out of the car and lit a cigarette. Smoke trailing from her hand, she kicked the shuttered garage door, and then a second time for good measure. After a few minutes, the small security door cracked open and a middle-aged man stuck his head out of the doorway, looking around the poorly lit lot somewhat blearily before spotting her and giving a heavy grunt.

"Oh," he said. "It's you. We were wondering what took you so long. Were you followed?"

"No," replied Pigeon.

He grunted again in response. "Come in," he said. "We're in the middle of a hand."

Pigeon flicked aside the butt and followed him through the doorway, letting the heavy door swing shut behind her with an ominous finality, and following close behind him as they snaked their way through the darkened garage, between cars propped up on hydraulic lifts or lying dead with their guts pulled out onto the floor. They went through another door, and Pigeon was confronted with a group of guys huddled around a table. Each person at the table was surrounded by a small clutter of cards, poker chips, and beers. An elderly sound system rested on a set of rusted metal shelves and pumped the sound of classic rock into the room.

Blueish smoke hung in a low haze around the ceiling. Someone had just told a joke, and everyone was still laughing. A pornographic calendar was tacked up on the wall above a CRT monitor and daisywheel printer. Next to that was a sign which read "Jesus wore a crown of thorns; ALL OTHERS, REMOVE HATS". Gerry absolutely despised people who wore hats in doors. Remembering this fact, Pigeon begrudgingly peeled off her knit touque, a cold chill settling over her bald head.

"Thanks," replied Gerry. He was a stocky man with a shaved head, no neck, and a short temper. Without looking up from his cards, he said, "It took you long enough. You weren't smoking in the car again, were you?"

"No," she said. "And I told you, that wasn't me. It was a smoker car."

"I don't want to hear excuses," he replied, adding "Okay, I'm up two hands, let's make this quick. You got what I sent you to get?"

"Yes," she replied.

"No complications?"

"No."

He squinted at her, as if trying to silently coax a confession of mendaciousness from her. She stared back at him, stony faced. After a few moments he nodded, seemingly convinced that she was telling the truth. He placed his cards face down on the table and leaned to the side, reaching into his jeans pocket to pull out a thick wad of cash.

He peeled off a small stack of bills and slipped the rest of the wad of cash back into his pocket. As she approached to take it from his hand, she noticed a few jealous eyes around the table fixating on the spot where the bank roll had disappeared. Pigeon wondered how much of the money that she was about to collect was being paid to her by the men sitting in the room now.

Taking the small stack of money into her hands, she riffled through it while the game resumed. When she reached the bottom of the pile, she felt a small sinking feeling in the pit of her stomach.

"I must have made a mistake," Pigeon muttered to herself, shuffling through it again. But no, she came up with the same number. She counted a third time, just to be sure.

"What the hell, Gerry?" she asked, perhaps a little more aggressively than she had intended. "Are you trying to lowball me?"

"No," Gerry replied without looking up from the game. "That's the going rate."

"This is almost half of what you paid for the last one," Pigeon responded indignantly.

"Older models are easy to get; the market is flooded with them, and they're cheap to begin with. What good are they? Parts, scrap, two-bit hoods that need a getaway for a stick-up job. The newer models have chip readers in the key-fobs; tools won't start 'em. Real Flash Gordon shit. That's where the money is nowadays: high end, wholesale, shipping overseas. The wall came down, and now those commie bastards can't get their hands on enough luxury cars."

"So what are you telling me?" asked Pigeon flatly.

"I'm telling you to count your blessings and be grateful for what you've got," said Gerry.

"There has to be a way to get at those newer cars," she said.

"You have to get someone to clone the chip. I can do it, but I don't think you could afford it."

"So I'm paying for the privilege of working for you now?"

"High end isn't my racket. I'm not looking to expand, and I'm not interested in taking on the extra risk."

"You don't trust me?"

"I just gave you cash for a job well done, sight-unseen. That's what trust looks like."

"There's nothing you can do for me?"

Gerry sighed, and said, "I tell you what: if you can get the cash together, give me a call and I'll see what I can do. Now tab out, Pig."

He pronounced her nickname with a hard 'G', a thing he knew that she absolutely hated. She turned on her heel and stormed out of the back room, jamming her touque around her ears as she burst out into the cold night air. Thin droplets of rain were starting to fall, caught in a halo of sodium light, glinting like shards of broken needles. She reached into her pocket and withdrew a cigarette and lighter. The storm may have passed, but it never stopped raining in Vancouver.

She had just about finished her cigarette and was considering chaining a second one off of the first when the metal door behind her burst open and Frankie, one of the older guys, stumbled out into the parking lot.

"I heard you needed cash," he slurred. "You wanna make a few extra buck, give me a ride home. I'm too flat-lined to drive. Get my car, it's around back." He drunkly shoved his keys into her hand.

Matching the keychain with the make, Pigeon slipped into the driver's seat of an early model sports sedan. Frankie slid in beside her, instantly filling the car with the smell of cheap booze and cheaper cologne.

"Where am I taking you?" asked Pigeon.

"We can do it right here, baby," he mumbled, sliding his hand down her inner thigh.

"She's a slut," said a voice.

"She's a whore," said another,

"She should kill herself," chimed in a third.

"Hell no," she said, elbowing him off of her.

"Flat," said Frankie, slumping against the window. "Take me to Jessica's place. She's always down."

He rattled off the address, somewhere in North Van, and Pigeon gunned the engine, merging onto the highway. The sooner she could stop playing taxi driver to this slob, the better. Luckily, he spent most of the car ride engrossed in his phone.

"We're here," she said finally, wheeling into the parking lot of the condo complex.

"Thanks, baby," said Frankie. With agility surprising for someone so inebriated, he lunged over the console at her, pinning her to the seat, and dropped his hand down her shirt. His tongue flicked out like a lizard and he aimed it right for her mouth, which had dropped open in shock. It took her a moment to get over the sheer surprise of the thing, by which time his tongue had slithered down her throat like a grimy, noxious worm. She bit down on it as hard as she could and he jumped back with a yelp.

Firing a quick fist into his kidney, she shoved him the rest of the way off her. His head hit the passenger-side window with a hollow pop.

"Oh, you flat!" he screamed, throwing his phone at her head. "I don't need this! I got bitches on speed dial!"

After clawing at the door for a few moments he finally got it open, half falling out of the car and almost landing in a sizable puddle. "I don't need this!" he repeated, staggering over to building's front door. Pigeon didn't wait to see whether he made his inside, instead squealing the car's tires as she peeled out onto the street. It took her a moment to realise that he hadn't paid her what she had been promised. She swore under her breath. She needed that money.

Sighing deeply, she got back onto the freeway. She would have to drop Frankie's car back at Gerry's garage, and then figure out her life from there. She was about halfway to her destination when an odd beeping noise began emanating from under her seat. At first she ignored it; if the voices were back, a few odd noises weren't out of the ordinary either. However, after a brief moment of silence it started up again. Concerned, Pigeon pulled the car over to the side of the road and started fishing under the seat.

She touched something small and vibrating and pulled out Frankie's cellphone. It seemed to be the source of the beeping, and the screen was lit up with the word "Donald" splashed across it. Unsure of what to do, she hit the big green button and brought the device up to her ear.

"Hello?" said Pigeon uncertainly.

"Oh," said Don. "It's you. Put Frankie on."

"Frankie isn't here. He threw this thing at me and stormed off. Without paying," she added quickly.

"Doesn't surprise me," scoffed Don. "He's sort of an asshole."

The voices:

"Don't trust him."

"You can't trust him."

"He knows what you are."

"He wants you dead."

"He wants your secrets."

"You're not safe."

"He can hear your thoughts."

"Listen," Don continued, "I had work for Frankie but Gerry says I can trust you so maybe this can work."

"This can work," said Pigeon shortly.

"Good," said Don. "Do you have a car?"

"I'm borrowing Frankie's ride," she replied.

"I'll tell him I need it for a thing. He'll understand. You know Nunya's? The diner on Main and 1st?" Don asked.

"Yes," said Pigeon.

"Good," replied Don. "Meet me there tomorrow evening. We'll talk."

"What should I do about this phone?" asked Pigeon.

"Keep it," replied Don without hesitating. "Sounds like that little creep owes you. His uncle can buy him a new one. Consider yourselves even." Then he hung up.

Pigeon slid the phone into her jacket pocket and pulled on to the next closest exit to Downtown. She swung the car into her pharmacist's parking lot and dropped the seat into recline. A billboard hologram cast an eerie glow over the empty swath on pavement, a rolling advert for a service that offered sex-for-money with anatomically exaggerated 'droids. Tomorrow would be a new day, thought Pigeon as she fell into an uneasy sleep. The billboard rolled over again, a single word splashed across it:

"Freedom"

CHAPTER 3
WHEN IT RAINS

Pigeon awoke to the sun starting its slow crawl towards the horizon, the smog burning orange below a thick layer of low rain clouds. A cool wind blew some leaves and pieces of trash across the parking lot, now partially full. She had slept most of the day, and there was an odd buzzing in her head. The voices had merged into one single droning monotone that was narrating her every motion.

She's looking around the car now. She's noticing the pair of panties stuffed under the passenger seat. She's thinking of Frankie. She remembers the phone she acquired last night. She's patting her self-down. She found the money that Gerry had paid her. She's getting out of the car. She's walking towards the pharmacy…

"Typify Eternna," said the little man behind the counter, reading the total off the cash register and holding out his hand. Pigeon grumbled, forking over the last of her cash. "PharmaCorp renewed the patent on tritipine, which means prices are going up for the injectable and the pill form, which means the costs are getting passed on to the consumer."

He pressed the airhypo to her skin, and it gave a pneumatic hiss as it deposited its payload of medicine into her upper arm. "Of course, most people are covered. But if you want to stay outside the System…"

"It's pay to play," said Pigeon, finishing his sentence, taking the handful of pills he offered her. Pigeon worked up some saliva by sucking the inside of her mouth and swallowed them in a single gulp. She started feeling drowsy almost immediately, more of a placebo effect than anything. She knew from experience that the real sedation would start in about half an hour, and that the only way through was to sleep it off.

"See you soon!" said the pharmacist as Pigeon left the small shop, door jingling cheerfully behind her.

Back in the car, she fiddled with her new phone until she found the alarm. Setting it to go off a few hours before she was due to meet with Don, she laid back in the seat and closed her eyes, allowing the drugs to take effect. Everything around her felt small, and she felt floaty and distant. The voice commented on this, but she ignored it. Soon, things would be quiet and she could focus on getting her life back together after this terribly botched Run.

It was raining again when she pulled into Nunya's rear parking lot. The meds were still taking effect, but the voices had already been reduced to whispers, nattering back and forth. She was still tired, though, sleep dragging her eyelids down. She had almost run two red lights on her way there, and came far too close to rear-ending a cop car. Luckily, she had made it there in one piece and some coffee would be perfect for slicing through the sedation.

"Glad you made it," said Don as she slid into the booth. By some coincidence, it was the same booth that she had sat at just a few days previous. Had it been a few days? Or a few weeks? Pigeon couldn't quite recall. There was a girl at the table too, dressed in dirty plaid flannel with lank, dirty-blonde hair

"This is Kim. She's a friend of mine. Kim's an old hand, so you'll be taking direction from her." The girl flashed a piece sign lazily over her coffee mug. "Pigeon here is new," continued Don, "so I expect you two to be on your best behaviour while you're showing her the ropes."

"The job is simple," said Kim. "In and out, no more than two minutes. I'm on cash detail, which means I ride shotgun and I do all the talking. Don't get twitchy; we don't need any bodies piling up on a job this simple. I have a getaway car; you'll be outside waiting for me to make the jump. Don says you have a ride?" Pigeon nodded. "Good. Once we're a few blocks away, we ditch the getaway and switch to yours. We're not safe until we bail out of the neighbourhood."

Pigeon motioned to the waitress, who filled a mug with coffee and slid it in front of her. "Seems simple enough," she said, yawning. "I'm in."

"This thing is for insurance reasons only. Split two ways less my taste, flat rate. So Pigeon, I expect this to be clean. Like Kim said, no bodies. And no yawning when you're on the clock. Got it?"

"Yes, sir," said Pigeon, stifling another yawn.

"Good," said Don. "Now, everyone chip in on this bill. I don't tip."

****

"Can I buy one off of you?" said Kim, appearing behind her unexpectedly, giving Pigeon a little start.

"Don't sneak up on me like that," said Pigeon. "Here, just take it," she added, handing Kim a cigarette.

"Thanks," said Kim, producing a lighter from the breast pocket of her shirt. "You know, Don's a misogynistic piece of shit. But he pays well, so I'm sort of stuck with him." Pigeon nodded, and Kim continued. "Don't get me wrong, I'm not in this for material gain. Any money I make goes to a better cause. Have you ever heard of the Skeleton Army?"

"No, never," said Pigeon truthfully, shaking her head. She was exhausted, the medication still working its magic. She just wanted this conversation to end so she could take another nap in the car.

"We do a lot of organising in the community, but some of our bigger projects need funding."

"Right," said Pigeon flatly. Why won't this girl leave me alone? she thought.

"You know," Kim added thoughtfully, "you and I are a lot alike. We're both women in a man's world. And we need to look out for each other, have each other's backs. You know?" Pigeon nodded hesitantly. "Do you have a phone? Let me give you my number." She pulled a cellphone from her pocket and tapped it against Pigeon's, which gave a little ping. "If you ever want to talk women's lib, or any kind of politics, give me a shout. We're sisters and we're in this thing together, okay?"

Pigeon nodded again, stubbing her butt out on the bottom of her shoe. Kim flashed her another peace sign again and smiled broadly. Pigeon noticed that she was missing a lot of teeth, and that the ones she had were very crooked. Without another word Kim turned and disappeared into the rain, leaving Pigeon alone and rather confused.

****

Despite her slightly odd interpersonal manner, Kim was in fact an old hand at armed robbery. Don's tip off had been solid, and the entire job went off without a hitch. After Pigeon was instructed to give back Frankie's car, she realised that she had nowhere to sleep. After spending a couple of nights curled up in the alcove outside the pharmacy, she responded to a couch-surfing ad in the classified section, paid in cash.

The robbery hadn't given her enough to replace her modded chip, let alone shell out for Gerry's fancy new car theft gizmo. So that was how she spent her time: sleeping the day away in the living room of the basement suite that she shared with four other people and working all night long. Cheap cars were easy enough to come by, and Gerry was always happy to take on more stock. Meanwhile, she was becoming closer with Kim, who was always looking to knock over another convenience store or gas station.

In return, she had to put up with Kim's political diatribes. Pigeon tended not to keep up with the news (she trusted SYSLink as far as she could throw it, the whole network another tool of the System, so far as she was concerned), so she rarely contributed much to these conversations. Kim, however, seemed more than content to monologue uninterrupted. Pigeon had never met someone quite like Kim before. She wasn't a Runner, but instead burned bright with self-righteous indignation, seemingly able to turn any issue into a black-and-white conflict between ultimate good and abhorrent evil. Pigeon had described her to Maria over coffee at her new place, and she had described Kim as Robin Hood turned *G.I. Joe*, a characterisation that Pigeon thought was far too accurate.

Despite her willingness to discuss her beliefs, Kim rarely talked about her personal life. Ordinarily this wouldn't have bothered Pigeon, who tended to insulate herself from most people, and tried to ask as few questions of people as possible. Better not to be saddled with the burden of becoming attached to people; a Runner technique as old as the first Run.

However, Pigeon found herself drawn inexorably to Kim. More than anything, she desperately wanted to know more about the

Skeleton Army that Kim had alluded to so cryptically in their first meeting. Finally, after they had been working together for what seemed to Pigeon like an eternity, she could contain her curiosity no longer. Cutting Kim off in the middle of rant about prison abolition, she blurted out, "So what the hell is the Skeleton Army?" Kim looked taken aback, staring at Pigeon as if surprised to see that there was someone in the car with her.

"Well," said Kim deliberately, weighing every word. "The Skeleton Army is a political movement based on the principles of voluntary participation and mutual aid."

"In English?" said Pigeon, giving her a hard time.

"Well, it's everything that I've been talking to you about, really," responded Kim evasively. "We provide an alternative to mainstream politics." With that, she shifted the conversation to an article she had read in some obscure zine, railing against the evils of hydro-electric megaprojects. Feeling decidedly unsatisfied with the response, Pigeon settled back in her seat. What sort of political movement was funded by armed robbery? she wondered.

By the time Kim dropped Pigeon off at home the sun was just starting to rise. They had been casing a liquor store for their next job, and Pigeon was too exhausted to pay attention to the slip of paper tacked to the front door. She figured it was just some bill collector after one of her roommates, and besides which she couldn't read it in the early-morning gloom. She didn't have the energy to take her shoes or coat off, instead flopping down onto the couch fully clothed, thoughts racing. Her roommates usually awoke around this time, so she wasn't expecting to fall asleep immediately anyways; they were archetypal Squatters, and they tended to give her a wide berth.

Thus, she was startled when a voice hesitantly spoke her name aloud from the shadows as the floor lamp clicked on dramatically. She was halfway towards reaching for the knife that she kept under her pillow when she realised it was one of her roommates and let her arm drop.

"Jesus," she said, breathing a sigh of relief. "Don't do that to me."

"Sorry," he said, "but we need to talk." Pigeon noticed that he was shifting uncomfortably in his seat, as if this was a task he had been put up to and didn't particularly relish.

"Okay," she said tersely, dragging herself up to a seated position, her joints groaning in protest. "What's the scan?"

"The police were here last night asking about you, and we are concerned that you are involved in… criminal activities." He spoke with the hesitant reverence better suited to addressing a cult leader or mass murderer than sort of petty thief that Pigeon was. She rolled her eyes, so hard that she thought they might unscrew themselves and fall out onto the floor.

"No, Tim, I'm not involved in 'criminal activities'," she said, a little exasperated. This lie seemed to put him somewhat at ease, so she continued. "What did you tell them?"

"We told them the truth," bragged Tim.

"Being?" asked Pigeon.

"Being that we hardly saw you at night and never talked to you during the day," he responded. Pigeon breathed another sigh of relief and flopped back down onto the couch, covering her eyes with the crook of her elbow.

"Anything else?" she mumbled.

"Well," he said, suddenly hesitant again. "You have to be out of here by the end of the week…"

"What?" exclaimed Pigeon, sitting upright again. "You're kicking me out over this?" Tim stared at her blank-faced for a moment before replying.

"You didn't read the notice on the front door?" he asked, dumbfounded. Pigeon shook her head no. "We're being evicted. The landlord is renovating the place, and he wants us out." With that, he stood up, threw on his coat, and left for work.

"Jesus," Pigeon mumbled to herself, grabbing her bag out from under the couch. She was almost too exhausted to move, but if the cops had been here once, they could come back at any time. She needed to get moving. More than that, she needed to figure out how they kept picking up her trail. Had she become sloppy? Complacent? She didn't think so, but at the moment she was too tired to reason it out.

First sleep, then she could play detective. Swiping a blanket off of Tim's bed on her way out the door, she built herself a little nest in the backseat of a stolen car, where she finally managed to drift into an uneasy sleep, lulled by the light patter of rain on the roof, and haunted by dreams of her parents' faces.

She awoke with a start, the reality of situation hitting her suddenly like a tonne of bricks: she was being hunted. So far, she had managed to evade the System through nothing more than luck, and her Runner's sense told her that her luck had run out. She needed to get to the bottom of this mystery, and quick.

The thought of Detective Pendleton's hungry blue eyes spurring her on, she clambered over the back seat of the car and slid into the driver's seat. Grinding the sleep out of her eyes with the palms of her hands, she willed her brain to start churning. After a few minutes, a thought popped into her head.

"Who," she asked herself, "knew about my couch surfing?" Aside from her roommates, she knew there were only two possibilities. "Kim and Maria," she answered.

The nearest payphone was on the corner, and her first call was to Maria, the only phone number she had memorised. After letting it ring for what seemed like an eternity, she gave up trying to reach her. She was probably asleep anyways, at this time of day. Her next call was to Kim, copying the number off of her cell phone. She picked up after the third ring.

"Hello?" Kim said loudly. There were a lot of voices in the background. It sounded like she was at some sort of party.

"Kim, it's Pigeon," she said.

"Oh, hey. Listen, I'm just in the middle of a thing. Can we talk later?" said Kim.

"The cops were at my place last night," replied Pigeon.

"Oh, shit, are you okay?" asked Kim.

"Yeah, just a little rattled. Are we still on for tonight?" They had planned to do the robbery that evening.

"Oh, we probably shouldn't. Not until the heat comes off of you a little bit. Let's talk soon though, yeah?" said Kim.

"Yeah," said Pigeon. "Yeah, let's talk soon." After they hung up, Pigeon spent a minute mulling it over. Regardless of whether she was guilty or not, it made sense that Kim wouldn't want to be committing crimes with someone who might be under police surveillance. Gnawing at her bottom lip, she tried calling Maria again. Again, no answer. She swore under her breath. Between the two, she was more inclined to believe that Kim- brash, opinionated, outspoken Kim- was the rat. More so than Maria, especially, who was the closest thing in the world she had to family.

Still though, she felt the need to confront her. She needed to know who she could trust, and if Maria happened to lose a few minutes of sleep to assuage her doubts, then so be it. As soon as Pigeon arrived at Maria's apartment, though, she could tell that something was wrong. Maria was a light sleeper, and yet there was a bar of light under the door and the sound of muffled music.

Pigeon pounded on the door with her fist, calling her name. After several minutes without any response, Pigeon made up her mind. Taking a deep breath, she started kicking at the door, right near the knob: once, twice. On the third kick, the lock finally gave way in a shower of splinters, and the door came flying open.

"Maria!" shouted Pigeon at the top of her lungs. Still no answer. Right away, she noticed the coffee sitting on the kitchen table. Pigeon touched the side of the mugs: still warm. Someone had been here recently. She called Maria's name again. There was no response, only the music. Following it to its source led her to Maria's bedroom. The door was ajar, and she opened it cautiously, preparing for the worst.

She was met with a grotesque tableau: Maria, unconscious and sprawled out on her bed, surrounded by piles of cash and empty blister packs. An expensive sound system was resting on the floor next to her. A small wad of bills lay under her head like a pillow, a rectangular piece of paper resting on top. As Pigeon drew closer, she saw that it was not a scrap of paper, but a business card.

The VPD logo glared up at her, beneath it was some contact information, as well as the words 'Detective Pendleton'.

Pigeon inhaled sharply through gritted teeth. Her heart was pounding so hard in her chest that she could hear it, thought that it might explode. Kneeling next to the stereo, she turned the dial until the music was at an intolerable volume that drowned out the frantic beating of her heart. Maria didn't stir, didn't so much as a flinch.

Crouching over Maria's listless body, a single tear welled up in each eye. She wiped them away with her index finger and took a deep breath, trying ineffectually to harden her heart. She drew her switchblade, the point of the knife hovering over Maria's throat, tracing circles over her heart. A feeling of darkness welled up inside of her, her Runner's Sense screaming at her.

Do it. Do it now. Make it quick. She couldn't. Not Maria. Not like this. She wanted to leave, but the pile of cash was too tempting. Stuffing bills into her pocket, she hesitated momentarily before deciding to take Pendleton's card. She wanted Maria to know that she knew.

"Au revoir," she whispered in her ear, planted a kiss on her forehead. *Until we see again.* Maria stirred in her sleep, but didn't awake.

Pigeon took the fire exit stairs two at a time until she was in parking lot, where a torrential downpour soaked her through almost instantaneously. Throwing herself into her beat up old car, she struggled to keep her composure. She needed to talk to someone. But who did she have left?

CHAPTER 4
THE GREEN ROOM

"Hey," answered Kim, picking up on the first ring. "Sorry I couldn't talk earlier. I had-"

"A thing," interrupted Pigeon. "Yeah, you said."

"Yeah," replied Kim. "So what's up?"

"The heat is off," said Pigeon flatly.

"Do you want to talk about it?" asked Kim.

"No," said Pigeon, "but I need somewhere to stay."

"You can stay with me," said Kim without hesitating. "I'm just on the East side."

Pigeon hung up the phone. Sitting alone, listening to rain hammer the roof of the car, she struggled to hold herself together, fingers tapping the steering wheel rhythmically. After a few moments, though, she could no longer manage. Letting out a low moan, she broke down dry-sobbing. There were no tears.

Pigeon had briefly explained the situation with Maria, and Kim was careful not to ask too many questions. At the end of the conversation, they both agreed that it would be better if Pigeon laid low for the time being. So, with some discomfort, she settled into a new domestic routine.

Living with Kim, Pigeon got to see a whole other side of her that was quite unlike the spunky, outgoing attitude that she had gotten used to.

While Pigeon would describe her own sleep pattern as 'nocturnal', Kim's lifestyle was something approaching truly erratic. She would stay awake for three or four days straight, during which she was a constant whirlwind of activity, planning robberies and ranting aloud about various political subjects.

Then she would crash for just as long, becoming moody and sullen, spending most of her time in bed or abusing inanimate objects. Pigeon learned to match the ebb and flow of Kim's emotions, cooking and cleaning with her on the good days, and sitting alone planning her next Run or inventing errands to run on the bad days.

Thus it was that on one of Kim's good days that they were smoking together on the patio. The back door was open, and the sound of one of Kim's punk albums drifted over them, mingling with the sound of the rain.

Kim smoked ultra-lights; Pigeon thought that there would have been more nicotine if they had been rolled with pencil shavings, but she bummed one regardless.

"So," said Kim, exhaling.

"So," replied Pigeon.

"I have our meeting tonight, and I was wondering if maybe you wanted to come this time?" asked Kim. Every Friday evening, regardless of her mood, Kim left for a mysterious 'meeting' and didn't return for several hours. She never shared the exact nature of these meetings with Pigeon, and she knew better than to ask, so the sudden invitation caught her slightly off guard.

Her mind was split. Her Runner's sense cried out overwhelmingly, screaming for her to not get involved. Her curiosity, however, was more than just a little piqued. As she mulled it over, she toyed nervously with the little metal scorpion. She had found it again while she was unpacking her stuff, and she had taken to playing with it absentmindedly.

"Hey, that's a cool little thing," said Kim. "What is it?"

"Well," said Pigeon, glad for the change of topic. "It was a little scorpion. But it kind of got... mushed."

"Aww," responded Kim. "How come?" Pigeon had to think about that for a couple seconds. Why had she started to untwine it? It seemed like centuries had passed since the little thing had passed into her possession.

"There was a thing inside of it," said Pigeon after searching her memories.

"Oh?" said Kim inquisitively. "What sort of thing?"

"Hold on," said Pigeon, hurrying to her room. Where had it ended up? She knew she wouldn't have thrown it away, not after all the trouble she had gone through to end up with it in her possession. After tossing most of stuff around trying to find it, she eventually discovered it at the bottom of the pockets of a pair of torn old jeans.

"Here," she said, sliding it across the table at Kim, who was waiting patiently.

"Weird," she said thoughtfully, turning it over in her right hand while using her left to smoke. "I've never seen anything like this. You?"

"No," said Pigeon truthfully. "Never. Can I bum another smoke?"

"Yeah, sure," said Kim absently, sliding the pack across the table to Pigeon. You know, I might know someone who can tell you more about this."

"Oh yeah?" said Pigeon, lighting up.

"If you come to the meeting tonight, I can introduce you," said Kim.

Pigeon hesitated, inspecting the embers dangling from her fingertips, even though she knew that she had already made up her mind.

"Edgy," she said finally. "Tab me in"

****

Stepping into Elizabeth's home was an immediate assault on all five senses. The first thing Pigeon noticed was how warm it was, the hot air rippling where it met the cold night, the scent of curry wafting through the doorway, so strong she could taste it. The next thing she observed was the loud reggae music playing on the record player against the far wall, and the posters that seemed to adorn every surface, slogans screaming as loud as the music.

No, that wasn't correct: on second glance, posters only covered part of the room. What really took up space were the books. More than anything else, the space was full of books. Shelves upon shelves of them, most of them with the covers torn off and the title scrawled in felt pen along the naked paper spines. In some places where there were no shelves they simply piled up on the floor. Not just in the main room, but Pigeon could also see some rooms in the back that were similarly packed full of books.

"Welcome," said Kim, shutting the door behind her, "to the Green Room."

Just then, a cooking timer on the stove rang. A middle-aged black woman with thick horn-rimmed glasses came bustling out of one the back rooms. Her tightly curly hair was piled on top of her head in a messy bun. She was wearing lime-green house slippers and pyjama pants that clashed horribly with her hot pink tank-top.

"Hi, Kim," she said in a heavy Jamaican accent, sliding a baking tray out of the oven. "And you must be Pigeon? Kim has told me a lot about you. Samosa?" She placed a plate full of fragrant doughy triangles on the kitchen table. Kim dutifully took a few off the plate and slid them into her purse before taking one for herself. Pigeon took one hesitantly, nibbling slightly at one of the corners. It was still piping hot, and the flavours exploded in her mouth, totally unlike anything she had tasted before. Seeing the expression on Pigeon's face, Elizabeth laughed warmly and offered her another, which she gratefully took.

"So," interjected Elizabeth, clapping her hands together over the sound of chewing. "Let's chat." They moved from the kitchen to the living room, where a number of lumpy, crooked couches sat in a semi-circle. Pigeon noticed that she walked with a distinctive limp in her left leg.

"Pigeon, Kim says you're reliable, and that you're looking for work," said Elizabeth, settling into a slightly threadbare armchair.

"That's right," said Pigeon through a mouthful of spicy potatoes.

"I have some products that need to be moved around," said Elizabeth.

"What's the heat?" asked Pigeon.

"My operation is pretty low key, and no one is trying to muscle in on our turf," responded Elizabeth. "Easy as can be."

"And the catch?" asked Pigeon.

"The catch," said Elizabeth, "is that I can't pay you much. I do most of my business by barter." If Elizabeth hadn't fed her already, Pigeon thought she probably would have walked out right then.

"We actually have a favour to ask you," interjected Kim, catching Pigeon's eye.

"Oh?" said Elizabeth inquisitively. Pigeon produced the little plastic chip, and Elizabeth took it into cupped hands.

"Interesting," she said, frowning. "I've never seen anything like this." Pigeon felt let down, and she shot Kim a glare. Kim missed it, however, waiting patiently for Elizabeth to speak again.

"Okay," Elizabeth said after about a minute of silence. "I think I know someone who can tell you more about this little doo-dad. Let's work out some sort of quid pro quo."

"Quid pro quo?" asked Pigeon.

"Right," said Elizabeth. "Information for services rendered. Deal?"

"Sounds good!" said Kim, speaking for the both of them.

"Great!" said Elizabeth. "Come with me, and I'll show you what the job is."

Slightly bewildered at what had just happened, Pigeon stuffed another samosa into her mouth and followed Kim and Elizabeth into the backyard. Elizabeth led them across a small tract of grass to a two-car garage, where she unlocked the heavy padlock protecting the door with an ornate key she produced from her pants pocket.

"They prefer the dark," Elizabeth aid in a

hushed voice as they stepped through the doorway.

As her eyes adjusted to the dim light, Pigeon could see that the garage was full of hanging troughs, all of them lined with small, luminescent mushrooms. As she watched, they shifted from blue to pink to green, and then back to blue. The pale lights shimmering against the roof of the garage reminded her of the northern lights.

"Wow!" whispered Kim softly. "I've never seen the grow before."

"What do you do with them?" asked Pigeon.

"Crush them up into tea," replied Elizabeth, ushering them out of the garage and closing the lock behind her. "They're great for chronic pain, anxiety, depression… I use them for my hip."

"What happened to your hip?" asked Pigeon.

"She had her pelvis fractured by a riot cop at a protest," said Kim reverentially.

"Right," said Elizabeth. "Once you find out what's on that thing, come back here and we'll figure out what to do next. In the meantime, let's get this meeting underway, shall we?"

"Pigeon, you're staying, yeah?" asked Kim, ushering them into the Green Room and shutting the door behind her.

"I came all this way, sure," said Pigeon.

"Great!" said Kim. "I'll introduce you." While they had been inspecting the garage, about a half dozen college kids had filed into the room, making themselves at home in the living room. All of them vaguely resembled Kim in some way, all grungy clothes and dyed hair. They were deep in conversation, but broke off when Kim called the meeting to order.

"We have a new recruit with us tonight, she's a good friend of mine. Let's all do our best to make sure she feels welcome." Pigeon flushed, and gave a small half-wave. She didn't like being put on the spot, but she was greeted by a lot of smiles and friendly waves back.

"First off," said Kim, "we need to discuss our finances. Then we should segue into a discussion of our ongoing anti-capitalist resistance tactics. Then I think we should discuss our operations in the suburbs, get an update on that. Is there anything else that we need to add to the agenda?"

There were a couple suggestions, including some updates on self-defence courses that they planned on running, and some discussion of a zine that they wanted to put out that would include details on how to hotwire old cars. Once the suggestions died down, Kim turned to the young man sitting next to her, Alastair, who was sitting with a battered, leather-bound note book. He rattled off some figures, numbers that Pigeon recognised as Kim's takes from their stick-ups together. After reading aloud the contents of the ledger, they began recounting all the acts of rebellion that they had engaged in since the last meeting.

It seemed to Pigeon like it was a constant game of one up-upping each other, starting with shoplifting and petty vandalism until they began to discuss more serious acts like arson and robbery. Kim seemed to win this little game, through a combination of subtle embellishment and the sheer volume of crimes that she and Pigeon had committed together. Finally, they came to the topic of a right-wing extremist group that was taking root in the suburbs of the city. They called themselves the Iconoclasts, but aside from the knowledge that they were prone to violence and originated in the prairies, they had little more to say. With that, the meeting was adjourned, and Pigeon turned to Kim, who was looking at her expectantly.

"So?" asked Kim, "what do you think?"

"It seems... different," said Pigeon hesitantly. "It seems like you do a lot of different things, but what is the Skeleton Army? Are you some sort of General? It seems like you're in charge."

"I'm flattered, but the Skeleton Army doesn't have leaders. At least, not in the traditional sense."

"How do you mean?"

"The Skeleton Army is a collective, which means that we make decisions as a group, by consensus. Like you just saw. Everyone is given an equal share of power."

"Okay. So you're a political movement...?"

"Right. We are a movement built on mutual aid and voluntary participation. No one is ever handed duties or issued orders; our members only do what they are willing and able to do."

"And what you do is... anti-capitalist resistance?"

"Correct. The original Skeleton Army was organised in the early 1880's as a lower-class movement against religious oppression. And we carry on that tradition through direct action."

"Direct action?"

"Right. We confront systems of oppression head-on, in the streets, where it matters most. Not in the classroom or the legislature, where our hands would be tied by the rules of the System."

"What's the goal? Like, what's the point?"

"To build a popular front of militant anti-capitalism. We are political, but we're not politicians. We don't believe in private property, and we don't waste time on pointless, endless debate. We take action. The power is with the people, and we hope to inspire people to take back power for themselves."

Pigeon sat in the corner, mulling over this new information, when Elizabeth approached her.

"So, you're ready to take on a work?"

"I'll tab in. What's the scan?"

"Simple. One big delivery, regulars of mine. Like I said, the heat should be minimal. The hand-off is at this address. When it's done, make your way down to Richmond. I know a person who can tell you more about what's on that chip"

"Then let's get it done. Kim, Elizabeth, I'll see you later."

****

After she had made the agreed upon deliveries, she followed the address on the back of Elizabeth's note, which brought her to a non-descript brick tenement in Richmond. Pigeon had to check a couple times to make sure that she was at the right place. Frowning, she flipped the paper over, trying to decipher Elizabeth's cramped, messy handwriting. Once she thought she had it figured out, she parked the car in the alleyway and walked around to the back of the building, where she knocked on the windowless door in the pattern that Elizabeth had described.

The door opened a crack, and a young man stuck his head out of the door. He looked around quickly, then ushered Pigeon inside. The first thing Pigeon noticed was the cold. It was a cool, wet day in Vancouver, but the antechamber was easily ten degrees colder than outside. Wordlessly, the young man began to pile on layers of winter clothing. Once he was done, he finally addressed Pigeon.

"You have the thing?" he asked plainly.

"The thing. Yes," replied Pigeon, handing him the little plastic chip.

He nodded, and then led her through the thick metal door to the inner chamber. A blast of cold air struck Pigeon in the face like an open-handed slap. If the previous room was like a refrigerator, then this one was more akin to a giant, walk-in freezer. The walls were lined with banks of computers, exposed circuit boards whirring with fans that almost drowned out the enormous cooling fans set into the ceiling.

"Computers are more efficient in the cold," said the Scribe by way of explanation. "They help him do his work."

The 'him' in question was laying in the

centre of the room in what looked to be an old dentist's chair set to full recline. Cables snaked from various computers around the room and plugged into a metal slot implanted in the base of his neck. A row of monitors sat across from him, flashing snippets of SYSLink reports and traffic cameras. An IV drip fed a constant stream colourless liquid into his bloodstream. This was one of the Watchers.

Pigeon had heard rumours about the existence of the Watchers, but she had dismissed them as just another urban legend. The way the story was told, Watchers were the antithesis of Runners. Whereas Runners evaded the System by existing outside of it, constantly trying to stay one step ahead of it, Watchers made themselves invisible to the System by allowing the System to subsume them entirely. The Scribe fed the chip into a console, hit a few keys on the keyboard, then settled down in an armchair next to the Watcher. He pulled a coil-bound notebook out from his jacket, pen at the ready, and waited.

Suddenly, the monitors flickered, the images replaced with lines of scrolling code. The Watcher began to twitch, eyes rolling behind closed lids, muttering softly. Pigeon couldn't make out what he was saying, but the young man hunched over his comatose form evidently could, and recorded everything dutifully in the notebook. As the page continued to fill up, she found herself steadily growing edgier. The anticipation of finally unravelling the mystery was killing her.

So when the Scribe finally presented the notebook page to her, she found herself greatly underwhelmed. It was mostly just gibberish, what seemed like random words, fragments of sentences, and nonsensical diagrams. At the very bottom of the page, however, was a single phrase that he had written in all capitals and circled many times:

A machine for ghosts.

The Scribe made a photocopy of the notebook page and handed the copy to Pigeon along with the small plastic sliver, both of which she tucked into her jacket pocket. Somewhat dejectedly, she made her way back to the Green Room, thoughts chasing each other around her head. Pigeon had to admit to herself that she had hoped for something with a little more pizzazz, like a map of the city with a big 'x marks the spot' with over the location of buried pirate gold. Or something. She really hoped that, for all of her books, Elizabeth would be able to shed some light on that mysterious phrase.

On the drive back to the Green Room, her cellphone rang.

"Hullo?" she answered.

"...Pigeon...?" Amidst the crackle of static, she was able to make out a single word. But that voice... It was impossible. Pigeon stared blankly at the handset. It couldn't have been Anita. Was she hallucinating again? Must have been. Anita was dead.

****

It was the summer of 1997. Late summer, hot, smog low in the sky. The only music on the radio was Big Shiny Tunes 2. The summer of '97. The year she met Anita.

Pigeon was working pizza delivery, with a little bit of weed on the side. She slept in her car, technically homeless, moving it from abandoned parking lot to abandon parking lot, constantly dodging the police.

Her same pair of torn black jeans and oversize white t-shirt were filthy, but she didn't have the change to spare for laundry services. She was trying to save up for her next dose, knowing all the while that the proverbial Sword of Damocles hovered over her head, the knowledge that at any point she could be made to disappear back into the CHEEK. So when she was fired, Pigeon found herself cast-off, cut loose and totally adrift.

The darkness, which had always been there, consumed her. A shadow that lived in her heart and devoured whatever joy she fed it. It had swallowed her whole. She couldn't afford her next dose on the amount of cash she had left in her pocket. Everything seemed hopeless.

Pigeon was sitting alone on a park bench in the hot sun, listening to the voices and chain smoking, idly contemplating the recent burns that dotted her arms, each one the perfect round circle of a lit cigarette tip. Her burgeoning Runner's Sense sent a tingle running up and down her neck, but she could do nothing to stop it.

"You should end it," said a voice beside her.

"You should escalate," said another.

"She should make it real," chimed in a third.

"She won't do it," commented the second voice.

"She's too weak," agreed the first.

"Hey baby," came a voice from behind her. "Mind if I sit with you?" Pigeon didn't respond. If she responded to every voice she heard, she would never stop babbling. The sun was in her eyes, and she couldn't immediately discern if this voice belonged to a real person or not. Evidently it did though, because a freckled, heroin gaunt young woman plopped down next to her, greasy red hair glinting in the sunlight.

"Do you hear them too?" she asked, after scouring Pigeon's face for a few silent minutes.

"What?" asked Pigeon incredulously.

"The voices, baby. Do you hear them too?"

CHAPTER 5
A MACHINE FOR GHOSTS

Pigeon arrived back at the Green Room, bursting with questions for Elizabeth. However, she was met with two bearded men wearing woodland camouflage and wrap-around sunglasses. The bulges under their jackets told her that they were armed. As she approached, they turned to face her, tension visible in the lines of their faces. Elizabeth was on the other side of the room, face to face with a young blonde woman in a red plaid jacket and heavy boots with the toes flayed open, revealing pitted metal plates. A hatchet hung from a loop on her belt. The air was charged; whoever this was, she was not a friend of Elizabeth's.

"Sorry, just gonna sneak by you,"

Pigeon said tersely, sidling between the two militia members.

"That's okay," said the blonde woman, staring into Elizabeth's eyes unblinkingly. "I was just leaving. Gonna leave you ladies to your little play date."

She turned to leave, but stopped in front of Pigeon. Squaring up to her, she gave her the same intense stare that she had been giving Elizabeth. Her eyes were a deep blue, the colour of a gas stove, flecked through with coal-black.

Pigeon had the uncomfortable feeling that this woman could read her thoughts, and cast her eyes aside. She turned to leave and the two militia men filed out after her, leaving Pigeon and Elizabeth alone.

"Who was that," asked Pigeon, "and what did she want?"

"I don't know," responded Elizabeth, peering through the blinds, "and I didn't ask. But I think that those were the Iconoclasts that Kim was talking about in our last meeting." Pigeon wasn't sure that was the whole truth, but she let it slide.

"I made your deliveries, and I saw the Watcher," said Pigeon, handing the paper bags full of cash to Elizabeth.

"Oh!" exclaimed Elizabeth. Evidently, she had forgotten about Pigeon's errand in the excitement. "What did he say?"

"A lot of nothing," said Pigeon dejectedly. "And this one phrase." She repeated it to Elizabeth, who frowned. "I was hoping you knew something about it."

"I can't say that I do," said Elizabeth. "Except…"

"Except?" prompted Pigeon. Elizabeth began searching the bookshelves, running her fingers along the spines as she talked.

"You know," she said, "more important than knowing things is knowing where to find the knowledge when you need it. Because knowledge is power."

"Kim said that that power is with people," said Pigeon.

"Kim is a good kid," responded Elizabeth hesitantly. "Her heart is in the right place. But where is her head at?"

"What do you mean?" asked Pigeon.

"Well," said Elizabeth, "Kim has a lot of privilege. She's white, thin, pretty, able-bodied, straight. She comes from a wealthy family. She can afford to play urban guerrilla. And her Skeleton Army, it's mostly just bored college kids looking for an excuse to vent their anger on acceptable targets."

"There's power in organising, yes," continued Elizabeth. "But unless you understand why you're organising, you'll never be able to create meaningful change. You'll never have a clear vision of what change looks like."

"On the one hand," Elizabeth concluded, "I definitely shared the animosity that the Skeleton Army had towards the System. On the other hand, I'm not as sure that lashing out at the System is necessarily the correct way to go about things. More importantly, I don't see how sporadic criminal activity will lead to the popular uprising that they seemed to think it will."

"But," said Pigeon, trying to keep up. "Even if you have all that knowledge, what do you do with it?"

"It's called pre-figurative politics. Do you know what that means?"

"No."

"It means that I try to build the world that I want to see, in my life time. The Green Room is an extension of that philosophy. We do food distribution, give people a place to stay overnight if they need one. Everything available for people to pay what they can, or trade what they have, including their time. Everything is done on a volunteer basis. We don't engage in violence, but we don't engage in traditional politics either. We exist outside the System, in preparation for a world without the System. You know?"

"Aha!" interjected Elizabeth, pulling a book off the shelf and handing it Pigeon. It was titled The Messiah Industrial Complex, by a Dr. Sophie Demarais, Ph.D.

She thumbed through it briefly while Elizabeth continued. "What do you do with the knowledge? You let it guide your actions, inform your values. If you only ever make decisions with your heart, you'll eventually find yourself straying to some dark places."

"Okay, then what am I supposed to do

with this knowledge?" asked Pigeon, tapping the spine of the book.

"Flip to the last chapter," said Elizabeth excitedly. Pigeon turned to the last page, where the running head identified it as belonging to a chapter called A Machine For Ghosts.

"Okay, so what?"

"Sophie is a Professor of Cyberethics for the Department of Computer Science at the University of British Columbia. We go way back. You should ask her what she knows about this Machine for Ghosts. But be careful. She's got something of a callous streak to her, that one, you know?"

"How so?"

"She holds the System in the same disregard that Kim or I would. But her ideas for overcoming the struggle are more… extreme. Personally, I think she sees humanity as little more than a petri dish for her experiments. If ever there was someone who would send in the tanks to enforce order, it would be her. Like I said, be careful around her."

****

The University was built on a peninsula that overlooked downtown, and Pigeon could hear gulls squalling in the distance as she approached the Computer Science building. The building itself was sheer white concrete, exposed aluminum, and glittering glass, an edifice to the ivory tower of academics. Pigeon grinned; she was still wearing her street clothes, and she looked forward to disturbing the bourgeois normalcy of the panorama.

Sitting in the waiting area, she was not disappointed. Every grad student that passed by was a perfect cookie-cutter image of the last, beige slacks and crisp polos, clutching books to their chest defensively, as if expecting her to lunge at them at any moment. Finally, her name was called and a slender, attractive young woman brought her up to Sophie's office.

She had her back to the door, so Pigeon knocked on the door frame and coughed softly to get her attention. When she turned around, Pigeon was shocked to see that she was a 'droid. Her soft blue synthskin and trailing optical processors marked her as an A Class.

Evidently this shock must have registered on her face, because Sophie said chidingly, "You weren't expecting a synthetic human, were you?"

"No," said Pigeon truthfully, caught off guard by the question. "I really wasn't."

"I don't have a lecture today, so you caught me just in time," she said, taking a seat behind her desk. "What can I do for you?"

"I have a question about your book," said Pigeon.

"You read my book?" inquired Sophie.

"Well," Pigeon shifted uncomfortably in her seat, suddenly aware of the fact that she had never finished reading a book that didn't have illustrations. "A friend told me about it. And I was wondering what you could tell me about the machine for ghosts."

"The machine for ghosts was a play on words, a reference to Koestler's critique of mind-body dualism, as a part of a dialectical approach to understanding wetware/software interrelations," said Sophie. Pigeon stared blankly at her, not having comprehended a single word that she had said. Mistaking her silence for quiet contemplation, she pressed on.

"The thesis was that the liberation of synthetic humans was dependent on the widespread acceptance of machine life by authentics, and the antithesis was that authentic liberation was dependent on the widespread acceptance of authentic life by synthetics. Therefore, liberation is dependent on a merging of authentic and synthetic, so that the ghost in the machine becomes a machine for ghosts."

"Okay," said Pigeon, nodding uncertainly. Clearly, she would have to be a little more specific. "Here's why I ask…" She then proceeded to explain, briefly, her encounter with the little sliver of plastic and how she had come across its contents. When she reached the end of the story, she heaved a deep sigh and looked across the desk at Sophie expectantly. Sophie leaned back in her chair, pitch black omni-eyes searching Pigeon's face.

"Can I show you something?" asked Sophie finally.

"Sure," said Pigeon hesitantly, Elizabeth's warning still fresh in her mind.

Sophie led Pigeon out of her office and down a series of hallways and staircases, each on as clean, well-lit, and identical as the last, with only the occasional black-and-white photograph trying in vain to break up the monotony.

"This is a clean room, so I'll need you to take certain precautions," said Sophie, indicating the white jumpsuits and clear facemasks lining the wall. Stripping off her outer layers, the small room filled with the scent of body odor and unwashed garments. Slightly embarrassed, Pigeon slid her slim frame into one of the clean suits, and strapped the respirator over her mouth. After a brief trip through the vacuum sealed airlock, Pigeon and Sophie stepped into the laboratory.

"Good-afternoon, Doctor. Would you like me to prepare a report on the animal trial?" A synthetic human- as 'droids apparently preferred to be called- greeted them almost immediately.

"Good-afternoon, Shelley," replied Sophie. "No, that won't be necessary." Shelley nodded, and turned back to observing the large maze that dominated the centre of the room. Pigeon peered over at it, apprehensively. She silently hoped that she wouldn't be expected to handle any of the rats that were currently working their way through the complex labyrinth.

"These rats," said Sophie, "have all been implanted with a neural graft that allows them to communicate to one another and share a single consciousness. Currently, they are exploring this maze as a single collective, and the reward for completing the maze will be shared equally amongst them. Meanwhile, Shelley is able to communicate with the collective, her goal being to offer a bird's eye perspective, guiding the collective in achieving its goal."

"Now," continued Sophie, "we can start to draw parallels between this experiment and the conditions that the System has produced. Under the System, synthetic humans are created to fulfil a purpose; as soon as we are born, our life has a quantitative value attached to it. Similarly, the displacement of authentic humans by synthetic intelligence also assumes a quantitative value on their life. You can see from the control group the competition between synthetic and authentic rats has created a hierarchical system of violence, whereas the experimental group functions with cohesion, guided towards a mutually beneficial result with precision and efficiency."

"Okay," said Pigeon, not even beginning to comprehend.

"The ghost is the collective consciousness, and the machine is the rats in the maze. And both the ghost and the machine profit, because they are working together rather than against each other, so that the System is irrelevant," said Sophie. "I hope this answers your question. Now if you'll excuse me, I have to prepare a lecture."

Pigeon had hardly stepped out of Sophie's laboratory when her cell phone rang.

"Good morning sunshine!" said a warm female voice on the other end.

"Who is this?" asked Pigeon, wandering aimlessly, looking for the building exit.

"Think of me as your deus ex machina," said the voice. "I'm putting together a team, and you come highly recommended. Let's talk in person." She rattled off the name of a hotel in Whistler, and then hung up. Pigeon stared at the receiver, dumbstruck.

****

Pigeon dropped the stolen car into park in the visitor's lot and checked the scrap of paper that she had written the address down on. This seemed like the place. Even more so than when meeting Sophie, Pigeon felt out of place. Whereas she had reveled in disrupting the homogeneous sterility of Sophie's laboratory, here she felt truly unwelcome, as if she had travelled to the edge of a medieval world map: here be dragons.

The elevator was on the opposite side of the lobby. Pigeon's shoes slapped hollowly against the marble floors, echoing in the cavernous space. Her Runner's Sense sent a prickle of electricity up her neck. She could feel a hundred gazes being drawn to her, and she felt more exposed than she ever had before. These people were agents of the System, hardwired to stamp out people like her at the mere sight of them. Grind them out, like a cigarette butt on the sidewalk.

The hotel suite was on the top floor, south facing. Pigeon took a deep breathe, and knocked on the door. After a few moments, a young woman in a black pantsuit and light gold blouse answered the door. Smiling broadly as she ushered Pigeon into the room, Pigeon noticed that she had too many teeth, each one a perfect, white square. She was reminded uncomfortably of a shark, bearing down on a wounded fish.

"Drink?" she asked, taking a bottle of sake off of the stove and pouring herself a glass.

Pigeon ignored the request, fully enamored with the view. Vancouver sprawled out in every direction, lights glittering through the few sparse rainclouds that drifted over the city like phantoms.

"It's beautiful, isn't it?" said the woman sidling up beside her. She swirled the drink thoughtful before taking a deep gulp. "Where are my manners? I haven't introduced myself. My name is Natsumi Kaji." She offered a hand to Pigeon, who took it limply in hers.

"Oh well," she said, grinning. "We'll work on the handshake. I suppose right about now you're wondering why I've brought you here."

"Yes," said Pigeon truthfully. Her Runner's Sense was screaming at her, begging her to back away slowly and Run forever. But something about Natsumi's warmth kept her rooted to the spot.

"Well," said Natsumi, swirling her drink. "I was serious. Earlier. On the phone. Do you know what deus ex machina means?" Pigeon shook her head, no. "It's latin, it means god from the machine. Do you understand?" Again, Pigeon shook her head no.

"Well, try to keep up. The System is a machine, and you can think of me as your God. I'm bound up in the System, same as you. The only difference is that I choose to make the System work for me, rather than letting my life be run by the System. Because your life is run by the System. Literally, I think. You Run, it chases. It chases, you Run." She paused. "I don't Run, because I don't have to. I am the System."

"And what," said Pigeon hesitantly, "does the System want with me?"

"So you're not as stupid as you look," said Natsumi, winking. "The System doesn't want you. You know that. But I need someone like you. Someone who thinks quick on their feet and who is as good behind the trigger as they are behind the wheel."

"That doesn't sound like the System I know," said Pigeon. "The System I know preys on conformity and listlessness."

"That's because I'm not the System you

know. I'm part of the new breed, les nouveous riches. Do you understand? The System you know is decaying; I make it my business to be in business. And insofar as that business is concerned, you can think of me as the reaper."

"What does the System want with me?" asked Pigeon again, more insistently this time.

"You've gone and pissed off a lot of people, and there's a price on your head. Whether you know it or not. And I've come to collect. If you don't want to end up washing ashore with your teeth and fingertips missing, you'll stick with me. Do that, and there will plenty more views like this one. So many, you'll be sick of them."

Natsumi reached into the pocket of her suit jacket, producing a wad of bills which she handed to Pigeon. Pigeon took them gently into the palm of her hand; based on weight and the denomination, this was more money than she had ever held at once.

"Congratulations. You are now a paid contractor of the Kuroyama Corporation. I'll have the paperwork sent to your new address."

"New address?" said Pigeon, still mesmerised by the money clutched tightly in her hands.

"The job comes with perks. Company residence, Company car." Natsumi wrinkled her nose in disgust, and added, "I suggest you get some new clothes. You stink."

"Thanks," responded Pigeon dryly.

"Oh, don't mention it," said Natsumi, grinning widely.

"Tell me more about this job," said Pigeon, slipping the wad of cash into her coat pocket.

"What," said Natsumi, draining the last of her drink, "do you know about the Millennium Project?" Pigeon thought hard, recalling something that she remembered Kim mentioning.

"It's a plan to gentrify the water front, right?" said Pigeon. Natsumi threw her head back and let out a bark-like laugh.

"In layman's terms, yes," said Natsumi, grinning. "Stick with me, and I'll bring you to the top of the world. When you're ready, you should meet the rest of the team." She handed Pigeon a business card with an address scrawled in ballpoint covering the back.

Pigeon flipped it over. Apparently, Natsumi was the Junior Vice President of Special Projects Division. The Kuroyama logo, a black triangle emblazoned over a hexagon, glared up at her. Pigeon's new identity beckoned her forwards. If she was going to sell her soul to the devil, she wanted to make sure she got the best deal possible.

"There is one thing…" said Pigeon.

"Oh?" asked Natsumi, cocking an eyebrow.

"The last time I 'got involved' with the System, they burned my chip."

"Oh!" exclaimed Natsumi, waving away the objection as if one would wave away a fly. "That's covered under your new medical plan. Get that sorted out right away. You might need it. After all, this is Pacific City."

"Isn't it though," responded Pigeon dryly.

CHAPTER 6
THE SALAMANDER AND THE HALBERD

"Hey, hey, hey! The usual?" said her pharmacist looking up at the sound of the door jingling.

"Actually Roberto, we're doing something a little different this month," said Pigeon, flashing her Kuroyama identification. "No cash, and I need a new chip."

"Sure thing," he said, slightly taken aback. "Moving up in the world, or something?"

"Or something," she sighed.

"What do want, chip wise?" he asked, preparing the injection. "The sky is the limit.

You ever want to speak Spanish?"

"I'll just take the basic, for now."

"Edgy," he said, over the hiss of the airhypo.

****

Following the handwritten directions brought Pigeon to the site of an abandoned factory in Port Coquitlam. As the heavy gate swung open, Pigeon thought she recognised the two bearded men that she had seen guarding the door at the Green Room, when Elizabeth had been confronted by the woman in red. Apparently, they were confident enough to openly display their firearms when they were on home turf.

Driving up the narrow gravel track towards the imposing brick structure, it occurred to Pigeon that everyone was proudly wielding some sort of weapon. She noticed too that the people milling about, or working the field, or exercising in groups, all had a lot in common. They were all white, male, young. Most of them had beards, and the rest all had heads shaved into pseudo-military styles. Everyone was wearing camouflage, hatchets dangling from loops on their hips.

She parked her car next to a line of pick-up trucks sporting oversized tires and got out nervously. Pigeon was uncomfortable around this many guns. Her Runner's Sense was screaming at her, making her painfully aware of just how vulnerable she was. She made sure to keep all of her motions slow and steady, just in case someone mistook her motives and had itchy trigger fingers.

She was greeted by yet another bearded young man with a long gun slung over his shoulder. "Pigeon?" he asked sharply. Pigeon nodded yes, afraid that if she spoke her voice would betray her nerves. "Welcome to Hell. Mother is waiting for you. I'll walk you in."

The deeper into the complex they walked, the more on edge Pigeon became. Finally, when she didn't think she could stand it any longer, they stopped in front of a steel security door. What she assumed was muffled music was blaring from the other side, although it sounded to Pigeon like someone was throttling a bullfrog.

"I'll wait here," said the man. "Go right on in."

Pigeon shouldered open the heavy door, and found herself in a large, windowless room full of exercise equipment. The sound system in the corner was blaring some heavy metal song, all shredded vocal cords and heavy guitar riffs. In the corner, a young woman with her white-blonde hair tied into a bun was working up a sweat on a rowing machine. Unsure of how to get her attention, Pigeon stood awkwardly off to one side, trying to catch her eye.

"I see you," she said breathlessly. "Let me finish these reps." She was wearing sweat pants and a sports bra, body glistening under the fluorescent lights, muscles tensing. Pigeon could see that her entire back was covered in a single tattoo: a salamander, coiled around a halberd.

The tail wove its way around her hips, front paws perched on her shoulders. The tip of the axe was partially covered by the hair at the base of her neck, and the blades snaked up the sides of her neck, ending just below her jaw. When she stepped off the machine, Pigeon could see a long, thick scar along her forearm. She brushed past Pigeon and killed the music, mopping her chest and face with a towel she had piled on top of the stereo.

"My name is Holly. You don't know it

yet, but I run this town. Do you know why I told Natsumi to bring you on-board?" asked Holly, slipping on a baggy, red flannel shirt.

"No," said Pigeon flatly. Holly turned and squared up to Pigeon, a large revolver dangling from her finger tips.

"Because you're a killer," said Holly, answering her own question. "I can see it in your eyes." She brought the revolver up and pointed it between Pigeon's eyes; Pigeon could see that it was loaded. She swallowed hard, but otherwise didn't react.

"And," continued Holly, "you're not afraid to die." She brought the gun up to her own temple and cocked the hammer, finger tensing on the trigger.

"Neither am I." She de-cocked the revolver and spun it around in her hand, handing it to Pigeon, who took it and tucked it into the waistband of her jeans.

"What do you know about our movement?" asked Holly, changing the subject. She indicated the large banner that dominated the wall behind her. It was crimson red with a splash of white in the centre, framing the silhouette of two axes crossed over a halberd that resembled the one that ran up Holly's spine.

"Nothing," said Pigeon truthfully. It was starting to occur to her that this militia was the far-right group that Kim had discussed at the Skeleton Army meeting. What had she called them then? The Iconoclasts.

"Drive for me," she said, shoving a set of keys at Pigeon, "and I'll show you."

The truck was stacked on a set of large, knobby tires, oversized suspension visible in the gap around the wheel wells. Pigeon struggled to make her way into the cab. She was glad that Holly had stopped to have a conversation with one of her men, because it spared her the indignity of having a witness to her embarrassment.

"This country is sick," said Holly when she was settled into her seat. Pigeon noticed that she didn't buckle her seat belt. "And this city is a tumour. You know, my daddy was a preacher. He built his church with his own two hands. That's the spirit that built this country. Now it's over-run with whores and thieves."

"Me, I make my money honestly," said Holly defiantly. "I know you take those pills.

What do you think is going to happen when the end comes? I'll tell you, you're not gonna be able to do jack. I don't smoke, don't drink, don't snort, don't pop. No chips; clean living, the way man was intended to live. All this," she said, gesturing widely, "all this lasts a hell of a lot shorter time than you might think.

"Now I've been to the other side," she said, indicating the large scar on her forearm. "Died and crossed over. My heart stopped beating for eight minutes before I was brought back. And do you know what I saw? Nothing. There is nothing waiting for us on the other side. The same nothing we come from. On that day, I stopped believing. And I started understanding. You know?"

Pigeon nodded. She wasn't sure she had grasped a single word that Holly had said. But there was a magnetism to Holly's cadence that made her feel like she had no choice but to agree.

"I own the single largest methamphetamine production facility in Western Canada. Drugs, guns, money. The perfect trifecta. But all of that is meaningless. Do you know why?" asked Holly.

"No," responded Pigeon.

"Because everything, and everyone, burns. The only true power is this." Holly held up a clenched fist. "Strength is power."

"Damn straight," said one of the men in the back seat.

"Alright," said Holly, as Pigeon turned out onto the main road. "We're going to Port Vancouver, loading bay nine."

After shuttling Holly around all day, Pigeon came to realise that she was less of a criminal and more of a savvy political operative. She spoke six languages, and conducted business in her customer's native language.

The drugs that Pigeon had delivered to the port were sold for cash, duffel bags stuffed to bursting with bills. The cash was driven deep into Chinatown, where it was exchanged for surplus Communist weapons, the serial numbers lovingly filed down to nothing.

These were returned to the compound, where a couple of young men with shaved heads unloaded the crates and disappeared them into the old factory building.

"Good," said Holly, sliding out of the

truck cab. "I'll tell Natsumi that you're reliable." She pushed a small stack of bills into Pigeon's hand. "For services rendered," she explained. Then she turned and too disappeared into the ominous brick fortress.

****

It was a few days later when Pigeon received another call from Natsumi. "It's time," she said, and then hung up. Pigeon yawned. She had fallen asleep on the couch again, fully clothed. The corporate apartment was secured with a state-of-the-art system, backed by a heavily armed concierge service. She was finally able to let her guard down.

For the first time in her life, Pigeon felt like a Squatter, and she didn't know what to do with herself. She desperately wanted to share this success with someone, anyone. But no one she knew would be willing to step into the hornet's nest the way that she had done. So, she had spent the last few days on the couch, sixty-inch television blaring trashy sitcoms.

On the drive over, Pigeon reviewed the plan in her head. It had been sent over in a thick manila envelope, delivered by an armed Company courier. "Assertive Corporate Espionage" claimed the header in typical

System doublespeak.

As near as Pigeon could tell, this was a classic armed robbery. Pulling into the gravel lot of Holly's compound, Pigeon immediately noticed that there were far more people milling about, armed guards posted in the upper windows, patrols lazily traversing the roof. However Holly's preaching sounded to Pigeon, it must be producing results.

The plan seemed simple enough: breaching into the basement, sweeping the immediate area, then ascending to the third floor where the safe was kept in a secure bedroom. Along the way they would expect moderate resistance, being sure to sweep and clear all hallways and rooms, not allowing any private security guards to get the drop on them. Whatever it was that they were after, Pigeon didn't know. Reams of technical data that she didn't understand. It also appeared as though some pages of the plan were missing. For instance, according to the blueprints that had been provided, the infiltration point was a solid concrete wall. She assumed, however, that Holly would know what to do, as her hyper-competence would suggest.

Rounding the back of the factory

complex, Pigeon could see a sprawling railyard filled with rusted out, derelict train cars. Holly was leaning against one of them, surrounded by a group of men in black ski masks. Pigeon pulled up alongside them and got out of her car, killing the engine and slipping the keys into her pocket.

"Good," said Holly, tossing her a mask. "We're all here." Pigeon slipped it on as Holly continued. "As some of you know, there are rail tunnels running all underneath this city. Our target runs parallel to one of these old tunnels." She dragged open the door of the boxcar she was leaning against, revealing a rusty, white, windowless van that had been modified to drive on train tracks.

"Our infil point," continued Holly, "is going to be a breach through the wall of the target building. After we set the charges, we're going to move with full aggression, through the basement and up to the main floor, clearing rooms along the way. We can expect moderate resistance, most likely armed guards. The intel is located on the third floor.

"Pigeon, we'll provide support and covering fire while your extract the intel. Then, we move back the way we came, exfil through the tunnel network. In and out, simple. No tripped alarms, no slip ups. Let's do this. Sic semper nihilim." Pigeon nodded, slipping on her mask, as the men around her returned echoed Holly's call to arms.

"Pigeon, you're in the back with me. We're oscar-mike!" shouted Holly, jumping into the back of the van, sliding the door shut once the last man had clambered aboard. The van began a slow rattling crawl along the rusted rail lines, picking up speed as the jury-rigged automobile slid beneath the face of the Earth.

"You've used a weapon before?" asked Holly.

****

"You see baby," said Anita, running her finger over the wet concrete. Her long fingernail left a divot in the soft, grey sludge as she painted. AZ + PS, surrounded by a heart with a little arrow stuck in it. "One day, the only memories of us will be the initials we carve for ourselves in the foundations of this city."

They sat next in that park all day, laughing and drinking beers, lounging in the shade, enjoying the heat. Anita's *Grizzlies* toque lay in front of them, next to a small cardboard sign extolling strangers for change.

Anita's shabby tenement. The window opened onto the roof of the next building door, and they were sat outdoors smoking and sharing a joint. It was a few weeks after they had met in the park, and they had moved in together, Pigeon's things light enough to be able to be packed into a single hockey bag.

"You see more than most people," said Anita. "You see the things that other people don't want to see, are too scared to see. They are afraid of you, because you see the truth."

"What truth do I see?

"You can feel the unreality of this world. You can feel us being watched, even right now, like someone is recording this conversation. Like, everything we do and say is leading us towards our destiny. Like everything is moving the way it should. Like clockwork"

Pigeon laughed out. "How high are you?" she asked, supressing another giggle.

"About six foot even," responded Anita, and they both howled with laughter.

****

Pigeon looked up at Holly. "This is Vancouver."

Holly nodded knowingly, then handed Pigeon an AK-patterned carbine assault rifle. An oversize scope was slung over the top of the hand guard, and an oversize muzzlebrake compensator hung from the tip of the barrel. She took the handful of magazines that Holly offered her and slipped them into the liner pocket of her suit jacket, along with two grenades.

"You still have the pistol I gave you?" asked Holly. Pigeon drew it from a shoulder holster and cracked the cylinder, revealing five .357 magnum rounds. Holly nodded, and dropped a handful of cartridges into Pigeon's out stretched hand.

"How does this sight work?" asked Pigeon, switching weapons back to the assault rifle. Holly leaned over, briefly running through its operation.

"The stock extends like this," she said, as Pigeon flipped the metal frame around in her hands. "5.56 by 39mm, magazine rocks into place, you charge it by reaching over the top like this." Pigeon worked the charging handle, coaxing an ominous clattering from the firearm and chambering a round. "The sight is digital, you switch it on here," Holly pressed a button, and a hologram projection of a crosshair appeared in the centre of the sight. It looked to Pigeon like someone had combined a digital alarm clock with a hunting rifle.

"Driver: halt," commanded Holly.

The truck rolled to a stop in another non-descript tunnel. Pigeon looked around quickly as she clambered out of the vehicle, but could see no indication that this was the particular section of filthy concrete wall that they were looking for. According to Holly's cartography skills, however, this was in fact the correct location, and so the loose collection of armed individuals fell into position, lining up single file against the wall that they were soon to come bursting through.

"Pigeon," snapped Holly, "you take point." She dutifully fell into the foremost position, hefting her carbine up against her shoulder.

Holly walked to the front of the line and placed a large bundle against the concrete, rubbing it into the gritty face of the tunnel of until it began to stick of its own accord. Pigeon recognised it as a plastic explosive, but had never seen it in such a quantity.

"Shaped charge," Holly muttered to Pigeon. "It'll punch through the wall no problem. There might be some backsplash. Watch your face. Don't disappoint me, Pig." She turned to the rest of the team and shouted, "Okay! Let's do this! Breaching on three." Sweat beaded on Pigeon's palms, slicking the wood furniture.

Time seemed to slow down as the breaching charge burst open like a deadly mushroom, imploding the wall against itself in a shower of dust, rubble, and sparks. Pigeon let out a wild, barbarian scream and charged through the newly created gap-

-and immediately came face to face with a man, the flesh seared away from his face, gasping for breath. Shrapnel wounds oozed and burned across his chest.

As he came gasping towards Pigeon, she noticed that most of his fingers were missing. She crosschecked the walking corpse with her machine gun, and it stumbled back against the wall behind it, finally collapsing in a gut wrenching gurgle. Pigeon was shoved forward as the men behind her in line began to file through; each shouted 'breaching' in turn.

Pigeon stood rooted to the spot, her heart pounding at her temples, eyes locked on the dead body before her.

"Clear!" Pigeon was shaken from the macabre scenario by Holly, patting her shoulder.

"Up to the first floor, move!" They stormed up the stairs single file, breaking off into two-man teams to sweep the empty rooms and shadowed corners, calling 'clear' as they went.

"Floor clear, second floor, move!" barked Holly. Pigeon, still shell-shocked, complied with the order, the pile carpeting squashing beneath her muddied tennis shoes. Spilling out into a well-lit marble foyer, they were suddenly met by a number of men in dark suits and darker shades, professional looking firearms at the ready.

"Contact!" screamed the first man to the top of the staircase, as his upper body was torn into bloody ribbons. The rest of them dove through the doorway, seeking cover as the bodyguards reloaded their weapons.

Holly's men and the guards exchanged a few volleys of gunfire before Pigeon worked up the nerve to fire a few rounds blindly over her shoulder. She was still quite shaken, and her cool Runner's demeanour was beginning to slide.

"Hey," said a voice over her shoulder. "Don't look. Too dangerous,"

"Shut up!" yelled Pigeon involuntarily, rolling onto her stomach and taking aim. The digital optic splashed across the chest of a guard, and she leaned into the trigger. The balcony railing in front of him shredded into a million tiny splinters, amidst sprays of blood from his bullet-riddled body.

"Hey," said the voice. "Excuse me,"

She rolled back into cover, as more volleys were exchanged and Holly's men gained the upper hand. Pigeon reloaded her empty magazine, rocking a fresh one into place and chambering a new round with a single satisfying motion. She breathed deep; some calm was beginning to be restored to her.

After the last few shots were exchanged, Holly ordered them to charge up the elaborately ornate main staircase. Dust hung in the air, shattered plaster and powder smoke. Pigeon was careful not to slip on the carpet of spent casings that covered the pockmarked marble floor. They encountered no additional resistance, so after sweeping the upper story, Holly's men took up defensive positions around the main office where the target was located.

The office door was locked, but it gave away after Holly punched it out with a deft swing of a very heavy axe. Cowering in the office was one remaining guard, who dropped his gun immediately upon seeing Holly and Pigeon.

"Please," he begged, "I have a fami-"

Holly took a swing at him with the back of the axe blade, catching him square in the stomach. He vomited explosively and dropped instantly to his knees. Choking up on the axe, she popped him in the side of the head, the sound of a coconut cracking.

Pigeon had to look away for a moment as Holly continued to deliver blows to the fallen man, blood splattering her chest and face. When she had filled her bloodlust, she leaned back on the axe, panting as her pupils dilated.

"Hey silly," said the voice. "You're starting to crack up,"

"Okay," said Holly breathlessly. "You're up, Pig,"

The vault was in the corner, a large black thing with an ominous strip of input jacks which glowed slightly green. The largest cord snaked across the floor and found its way into the personal computer sitting on the desk. Pigeon suddenly understood why her participation in this heist was so important: she recalled Holly telling her that cybernetic technology was forbidden as a part of one of her doctrines, something about the purity of the human spirit.

Pigeon lay down on the floor next to the safe, quickly snatching the cord running into the front input panel, moving it from the computer to the one on her left wrist. A vision swam before her eyes, crisp in the dark of the room: black velvety fabric, rippling softly behind a series of stacked rectangles. Focusing her will power, she shifted a portion of one rectangle to another so that they were of equal length. As she did so, another rectangle on the other side of the display increased in size. Pigeon grimaced: a puzzle. She hated puzzles. With a deep sigh, she began shuffling the rectangles around aimlessly, waiting for something to click into place.

When it eventually did she heaved another deep sigh, this time of relief. Unplugging from the safe, the digital display stained her eyes with purple spots as if she'd been starting into a too bright light, and she herself was a little lightheaded. She hated cyberspace, vastly preferring 'the meat'. As Pigeon clambered to her feet, Holly took a long swing at the safe with the axe. It connected just below the base of the door, and it set off a huge shower of electric sparks

"Booby-trap," Holly explained, getting down on her knees to open the safe. Inside sat a small metal plate. It looked eerily similar to the ones that Pigeon had been trying to move hot, when she had been double-crossed. "Package secured," shouted Holly. "Let's go home, people."

CHAPTER 7
THE KINGDOM OF DARKNESS

A rooftop holo lit the living room with an eerie, pale glow. Pigeon was sprawled on the couch, half awake, her fingers trailing limply over a pile of cash. The soft warmth of synthetic narcotics lulled her into a half-sleep. She imagined that this must have been how Maria had felt.

God, she just wanted out. Was that so much to ask? She could feel the silhouette of the shadow of Death encroaching on the edges of her consciousness, blurring her vision of reality like tears, stinging her eyes. Because, underneath it all, she could feel the abscess grow deeper. Her dreams were bleeding over into her memories, staining the fabric of reality.

The shadow was growing more incessant in its demands of her, urging her to slip further into darkness and closer towards some version of herself that she detested; a journey that she knew she may not survive…

She was interrupted from her delusional thoughts by her cellphone ringing.

"Hey," said Kim. "I haven't heard from you in a while." The words 'are you okay' never left her mouth, but Pigeon accepted this as a call of concern.

"Hey," responded Pigeon. "I've just been…" she trailed off. What had she been doing? She was so used to Running that all this standing still made her head spin, made her lose track of time, even more so than usual.

"Busy," said Kim. "Aren't we all?"

"Right," said Pigeon awkwardly.

"Listen," said Kim, "there's another meeting tonight. I heard a rumour you were running with a different crowd these days, but this is an important one and I was wondering-"

"I'll be there," said Pigeon. She needed

to get out of this damn apartment before it suffocated her.

****

"Fancy threads," said Alastair suspiciously as Pigeon stepped through the door way to the Green Room.

"Good to see you again," said Elizabeth from the couch. "There's a pot of gumbo on the stove, feel free to help yourself."

"Good-evening," said a soft voice from the corner. Peering around Elizabeth, Pigeon recognised Sophie, sitting in the corner, cold black eyes ever watchful.

"Hi," said Pigeon. This meeting seemed as important as Kim had said it was; this looked like it was all hands on deck. There were two people in the room that she didn't recognise, and they introduced themselves as Lynne and Cherry, respectively.

Once everyone had settled, Elizabeth spoke. "Now, the purpose of this meeting is to discuss the Millennium Project and our response to it."

Kim pulled out a map and unfolded it on the table in front of them.

"The Millennium Project will encompass most of this region," said Sophie, indicating the waterfront on the map." The population density in this region is calculated to triple within the next five quarters."

"The project isn't just about gentrifying the waterfront," said Pigeon, recalling what Natsumi and Holly had said.

"What?" asked Elizabeth, surprised. "What is it about?"

"I don't know," said Pigeon truthfully. "I've been… running with a different crowd lately. But it seems like everyone is trying to stake a claim on the Millennium." The room leaned back in their seats, processing this new information.

Alastair was the first to break the silence, eagerly producing a leather-bound notebook. "We've been tracking the operations of the Iconoclasts in the City," he paused to shoot Pigeon another suspicious look, who shifted uncomfortably in her seat. "And it seems like activity in the eastern part of the city is seeing a huge upswing. Not to mention the suburbs, where they've managed to patch over most of the local gangs."

"What we need," said Kim, "is a show of force. Show the System that we refuse to stand by and allow this to happen."

"I agree," said Elizabeth.

"The Skeleton Army is more than happy to run security," said Alastair proudly.

"I have an objection!" said Lynne. Everyone in the room shifted to face the speaker. "I don't think this group has taken into account Indigenous identity and land title. The waterfront has historically been Coast Salish territory."

"Yes!" exclaimed Cherry. "And I object to Sophie's presence here. She claims to be an anti-oppressive activist, but she benefits from colonialism as much as anyone!"

There was a loud objection from everyone else in the room before Elizabeth responded. "I object to that statement on the grounds that it is blatantly synthphobic."

"Synthphobic?" asked Pigeon.

"Open discrimination against synthetic humans," said Sophie. "I'm used to it,"

"I don't have a problem with her being a

'droid. My problem is with her writing. Have you read her books? She wants a robot revolution where humans get implanted with microchips like farm animals!" At the word 'droid, there was a collective intake of breath from everyone in the room.

"That's way offside," said Elizabeth.

"I agree with your analysis of Sophie's work," said Alastair, "but that's not an excuse to use a slur."

"I object to your slanted and narrow minded view of my work," said Sophie. "Empathy and efficiency can both be boosted through neurological-"

"Can I please bring the meeting back to the topic of decolonisation?" said Lynne.

At this point, Pigeon was thoroughly lost. Excusing herself as she stood up, she went outside for a smoke. Kim joined her, the two of them staring out into the rain.

"So," said Kim awkwardly.

"So?" asked Pigeon.

"This new crowd you've been running with. They're treating you okay?"

"Yes," said Pigeon. In the ensuing silence, she thought more on the question. How was she treated? She was certainly well paid and well looked after. But hadn't Elizabeth looked after her when she fed her? When Kim gave her a place to stay? Did they pay? No. But there was a generosity there, offering all that they had to give, a genuine warmth that was a far cry from Holly's cold ruthlessness and Natsumi's artificial personality.

And a guilt was gnawing at Pigeon's stomach that she couldn't quite place. A lesson she had learned from Anita, and Maria. She had thought of herself as an agent of death for so long, she had trouble remembering what it had been like to breath. She had been Running for so long, she had forgotten what it felt like to stand still. She had trouble believing that she would ever be free.

"You know," said Kim, breaking the silence. "If you're in too deep with these people, you should consider being our woman on the inside."

"What do you mean?"

"Give them a call, see what you can find out what their plans are," said Kim, grinding out her butt on the porch railing.

"Yeah," said Pigeon, doing the same. "Yeah, maybe I will."

****

Granville Street, the city's club district. Dirty brick and aged tile backed with neon and rooftop holos. Rain splattered around her as she parked the Company car on the side of the road. Darting across the sidewalk and into the nightclub, Pigeon was met with a flurry of construction.

"What do you think?" asked Natsumi. "We're gonna push the walls out, get some plush seating against the walls. Really trick out the VIP. It's gonna be high luxury, top quality stuff." Pigeon nodded uncertainly.

"No," continued Natsumi. "This isn't your of expertise. You're one of the killing people, people. Shoot stuff and blow things up, am I right? What's the matter sport, is my killer losing her edge?" Natsumi had seen Pigeon grimace at the mention of her body count.

"No," protested Pigeon. "It's just that I-"

"Hey, darling. Bare concrete, exposed wiring... I really like what you've done with the place."

Pigeon was spared having to come up with a plausible excuse when she was interrupted by Holly swaggering down the front stairs.

"You two know each other?" asked Pigeon as Holly and Natsumi exchanged a quick hug.

"Oh yeah," said Natsumi. "We go way back."

"We have the same alumnus," explained Holly.

"It means we went to the same university," said Natsumi.

"I know what an alumnus is," lied Pigeon.

"Bullshit," said Natsumi, calling Pigeon's bluff with a wide grin.

"Okay okay okay!" interrupted Holly. "Let's get down to business."

"Right," began Natsumi, "the purpose of this meeting is to coordinate strategies. Thanks to Holly's ingenuity, I have been able to acquire this formerly System-run piece of real estate."

"Now," she continued, "we've done a good job of breaking up the Mob's operations, and by some extension, the grasp of the System on power. The New Millennium is almost here. All we need to do now is deliver the killing blow."

"The Mob? The System? Explain," said Pigeon.

"Simple," said Natsumi. "The System is made up of three parts: the Party, the Companies, and the Mob. The Mob launders its money through the Companies, which donate politically to the Party, which in turn uses its influence to allow the Mob to continue operating, free from police interference."

"And you're attacking all three?" asked Pigeon.

"No," said Natsumi. "The Party is much too powerful to be confronted head on. But the Millennium Project won't be able to go ahead with the System fully intact. So we need to start 'work' on the two pillars that hold it up."

At this, Holly spoke up. "We've discussed our plans for the Millennium Project. And you know where I stand."

"Where do you stand?" asked Pigeon.

"Revenge," said Holly simply.

"As you can tell," said Natsumi, "Team Good Guys has been at loggerheads for a while."

"And I keep telling you. that's a ridiculous name for this so-called partnership," said Holly.

"Do you see what I have to deal with?" Natsumi asked Pigeon jokingly.

Natsumi and Holly exchanged another quick hug, before Holly said, "Okay Pig, you're on me. Let's get this done."

****

Holly had Pigeon drive her to an empty field in Surrey, their breath misting in the cold night air. A faint patter of rain set the grass twinkling in the low, light-pollution illuminated clouds. It was just the two of them, standing in the dark. Pigeon was nervous. She didn't know what was going to happen, but the thought of being alone with Holly for any amount of time set her on edge. More importantly, the lack of her usual entourage made Pigeon uncomfortable. How were the two of them meant to take on the mob in this little stretch of grass and dirt?

Too many unanswered questions, said her Runner's Sense.

After a few minutes, a late model luxury sedan pulled up to the opposite side of the field and four bodies piled out. As they approached, Pigeon's stomach dropped as she recognised Don. He was trailed by Frankie, and two older men she didn't recognise.

"This," whispered Holly to Pigeon in a quick aside, "is the mafia in Vancouver. The Russo and Catalano families."

"Oh, this is too good D, the snake and the rat," said Frankie as each party squared off against the other.

"Oh, we'll deal with her in a second," said Don, glaring at Pigeon. "You think you can steal from us, and I'm not gonna find out about it? You're dead, Pig."

"No, you fragged out real good, Pig," said Frankie. "Now, you and your friend here-"

There was a crack like whip and Frankie's face shattered into a mess of skull shards and brain matter.

"What the fu-?" asked one of the older men, before another whip crack stove his head in, too.

Pigeon noticed a strand of grass shifting, against the wind. Had she imagined it? No, the patch of grass was definitely moving. In a moment, it had taken human form as a man in a ghillie suit stood up, sniper rifle trained on the back of Don's head.

"You want to keep playing games, Catalano, or should I just shoot this piece of shit now?" Holly asked the other man.

"Mother's wishes!" confirmed the man with the rifle. Even from a distance, Pigeon could feel his cold gaze.

"Jesus Christ!" exclaimed Don, throwing his hands up in the air, the Catalano following suit.

"Did you really think you'd be able to walk into the hornets' nest unstung?" asked Holly as she approached the two helpless men.

She stopped a few millimetres from Catalano's face, squaring up against him, her cold blue eyes boring into his dark brown ones. After a few moments of frosty silence, something in her mind snapped and suddenly she was on top of Don, raining blows down on him with a hatchet. He squealed in pain and shock, almost pig-like.

Before Pigeon could react one way or the other, the old man was pulling Holly into a chokehold, handgun pressed against her temple. Don wheezed on the ground, blood pouring out of him like water from a broken main.

"Pigeon…" gasped Holly.

"Don't you make a fragging move!" shouted Catalano.

Without thinking, Pigeon had drawn her revolver. The old man shifted Holly to cover his centre of mass, as he began backing towards the car.

"Don't be stupid. You touch that trigger and I'll blow her fragging head off. You dumb flat, you're already dead, you just don't know it yet."

"Shoot me," Holly wheezed. "Kill him."

"When we meet again, you're in for a world of sh-"

Pigeon dropped her aim to the ground and leaned into the trigger. From close range, the heavy steel-coated round over-penetrated his foot, kicking up a cloud of mud and bloody severed tendons. Catalano let out a shrill cry and stumbled backwards, releasing Holly. She gave him a quick shove, before another whipcrack tore his knee cap out, blood splattering on Holly's chest.

Catalano collapsed to the ground, panting, unable to support his own weight. Holly reached to her waistband and pulled out a walkie-talkie. "We're clear. High value target is in custody. Send in your team."

A few moments later, a beat-up cube van pulled up alongside Holly's truck and several camouflage-clad young men jumped out. One of them was clutching what looked like a cross between an eggplant and a horse rein. The rest were wielding assault weapons of various makes and origins, each one moving with single minded intensity. Two of them hefted Catalano off the ground, slinging him over a rotting tree trunk while another two started binding him tightly with flexicuffs on his hands and feet. As they moved, Holly took the strap-on from the militia member and began stringing it on over her sweatpants.

"Pigeon," commanded Holly, "use your phone camera. Take a picture of this piece of shit, so that everyone knows how I take care of business."

A sick feeling began to work its way through Pigeon's stomach, her Runner's sense blaring an alarm in her head. She suspected what was coming, but hoped to God that it wouldn't play out like her imagination told her it would.

****

"Violent lives, ending violently," whispered Anita. "This is the world we've made for ourselves, babe. Part of us wants there to be light in the world. But deep down, part of us knows that there never will be. There used to be innocence in our lives. Now there's an abscess."

Pigeon nodded. The continuation of a conversation they had been having off and on over the last week. My god had it only been a week? It felt like years had passed since she had been saved, sitting in that park.

"I need you to understand baby, respect is everything. The only thing that matters is respect. Do you understand?"

Pigeon nodded again, as Anita produced a bulky tube from beneath the blanket.

"So baby, you know what you need to do, don'tcha?"

A light smattering of rain was beginning to fall as Pigeon stood across the street from the filthy brick tower. She was smoking a cigarette- for all she knew, her last one. The pistol Anita had given her was tucked into the waistband of her sweatpants.

Stamping the butt out against the bottom of her shoe, she crossed the street quickly, hoping to lose whoever was trying to follow her. Through the doors, past the empty concierge desk, up the stairs, two at a time. Floor number seven, room seven six eight. Two guards with stubby shotguns.

There had been other lessons over the last week. Anita knew a lot of people, and between all of them Pigeon had learned the basics of survival. Not the kind of survival she had been doing, but how to survive in the real world.

She had learned how to lift products in stores without being noticed. She learned how to jack and wire a car. How much caffeine to cut with heroin and horse-dewormer with cocaine. How to pick a lock. And, as was most relevant right now, how to shoot.

Walk towards them at the diagonal. Conceal the firearm until the last possible moment, the same way you'd lift a hard drive. Two shots, one to the base of each guard's neck.

They sort of shivered and toppled over, like poorly built snowmen. She snatched up one of the shotguns, flicked off the safety, cocked the weapon, and kicked open the door.

Two in the kitchenette: one, pump, two, pump.

A shot past her shoulder wizzes past, whining against a stud in the wall behind her. A third shot, catches him directly in the centre of his face, the skull imploding, turning itself inside out as teeth and grey matter splattered the bare wall behind him.

Pigeon dropped the shot gun and ran; ran until she was weeping, and snot dripped from her nose, her whole body on fire. She took the long way back to Anita's tenement, stopping under the illuminated EAST VAN cross for a cigarette. Sweat poured off of her, salty droplets getting lost in the rain.

Jesus. What had she just done?

****

When it was over, Catalano lay limply against the tree trunk, weeping openly. Pigeon was rooted to the spot, queasy. Stripping off the strap-on and handing it back to one of her militia members, Holly got down close to his face and hissed at him in a whisper.

"Now everyone is gonna know that you take it up the ass from women."

A light drizzle began to fall as Holly ordered her men to pack up and exfil the site.

"Pigeon, hold on to those pictures. That's all we're gonna need to keep this piece of shit in line. From now on, I run this town. Me. Meet me back at the club, and we'll discuss our next move."

The van drove off, leaving Pigeon alone with Frankie's weeping. When she could hold it back no more, Pigeon doubled over, vomit narrowly missing her feet. Shakily, she began to walk away, no particular destination in mind. She just needed to be away from this place.

The rain built steadily to a downpour as she walked, so that by the time she had made it a dozen blocks away she was drenched through to the bone, short hair plastered against her neck and forehead. Finding a dry alcove, she curled up into a ball, rocking back and forth as she wished aloud that she could just disappear. Her break down was interrupted by her phone ringing. Glad for the distraction, she answered on the second ring.

"Hello? Who is this?" she asked. Static on the line crackled.

"…Pigeon…"said a voice.

"Anita?" demanded Pigeon. "Anita, is that you?"

"Yes," said the voice weakly.

"Anita how is this possible? You're dead. I found you," said Pigeon.

"I don't know where I am. But I'm cold, and it's dark," said Anita.

"Anita," said Pigeon, tearing up. "Anita I'm scared."

"It'll be okay baby," said Anita. "I promise. But the Millennium is almost here.

And you need to stop it."

"Stop it?" asked Pigeon. "How?"

"Baby," said Anita. "I love you so much. Please…"

Static crackled on the line again, before the handset went dead in Pigeon's hands. She stared at dumbly, still soaked thorough with rain. She knew where she needed to go: back to where it had started, the park where she had met Anita, where they had carved their initials into the foundations of the city. Climbing the slippery steps of the SkyTrain station, she wasn't sure what had brought her back to this place. But she thought maybe that seeing it again would help to fill in some of the connections. When she arrived at the park, however, she found the whole thing was roped off. A crew of land surveyors had set up a small laser-level device, and were recording measurements on digital clipboards. A white van with the Kuroyama logo was parked a short distance away.

"Hey!" she said to one of the surveyors. "What the hell are you doing?"

"Lady, this area is off limits. You'd best clear out," responded the man without looking up from his notes.

Pigeon rummage around in her jacket pocket, producing a laminated Company ID.

"I work for the Company," she said assertively.

"Oh, sorry," he said, finally turning to face her. "I didn't realise. We're just following orders, you know the drill. Company wants this plot of land staked for the Millennium Project, we stake it. You know the drill," he added, repeating himself.

A prickle ran up her neck, her Runner's Sense telling her that she was being watched. She whipped around, nothing seemed out of place. Someone in a window perhaps? She checked the rooftops for silhouettes but saw none. There was a short line for the ATM, but no one was paying her any heed.

The feeling of being watched intensified. She needed to get out of this place.

****

When she arrived at the night club, the first thing that Pigeon noticed was that the construction was nearly finished. When she commented on this, Natsumi grinned broadly.

"See? Money is power, kiddo. When the work goes around the clock, it hardly takes any time at all."

Holly sat next to Natsumi in the VIP section, silently simmering with rage. They must have broken off an argument right before Pigeon arrived, and she was clearly itching to restart it.

"Listen," said Pigeon. She had made a stop at her apartment and had changed into something more casual, dark jeans and a baggy sweater. "I've been thinking-"

"That's a mistake," said Holly shortly. "What did I tell you? Thoughts rot your brain. They are the enemy of action. Don't think, just do."

"Right," said Pigeon. "That's what I wanted to talk to you about."

"Go ahead," said Natsumi. "Please ignore my compatriot's surly attitude."

"Well," began Pigeon, "you've had me working for you on this Millennium Project. But you've never explained why the Millennium is so important."

"The Millennium," said Natsumi,

choosing her words carefully, "is a very sensitive time. Do you know about the Y2K bug?"

"No," said Pigeon truthfully.

"At midnight on New Year's Eve, all the computers shut down," interjected Holly.

"Yes, essentially," confirmed Natsumi. "What that means for this City's power players is that there's a golden opportunity, a window, during which everything will be up for grabs. With the mob out of the way," she nodded at Pigeon, "that just leaves it up to Team Good Guys to divide the spoils."

"Which is where we appear to have reached an impasse," said Holly.

"Impasse?" asked Pigeon.

"It means we've reached a disagreement," explained Natsumi.

"I know what an impasse is," said Pigeon defensively. "What's the scan?"

"Natsumi thinks I'm taking things too far," began Holly.

"And Holly doesn't think I'm taking

things far enough," finished Natsumi.

"So what does that mean for me?" asked Pigeon.

"It means your loyalty is going to be tested," said Holly. "We've done a lot of good work together but this next step is going to take someone with ice in their veins."

Pigeon shifted uncomfortably. Images of Catalano, lashed to the tree trunk, flashed before her eyes, while Anita's ghostly warning ran through her head.

"Is there any way we can, you know, forestall the Millennium? Put the project on hold?" asked Pigeon.

"What's the matter?" chided Natsumi. "Is my killer finally having a change of heart?"

"I was just talking to some of the Company surveyors. This project," said Pigeon. "This project is going to affect me, personally."

"Exceptions can be made, compensation for loyal employees," responded Natsumi. "Yes, that's possible. But the Project is so much more than that. It's about creating a plutopia on the shores of the Pacific Ocean. A playground for the rich and famous, free from crime and filth and disease."

"Or," added Holly, "we take our anger to the streets, show the System we won't be pushed around any longer."

"Unless you've lost the stomach for the criminal lifestyle," said Natsumi, searching Pigeon's face.

"Well," began Pigeon, "the last job we did-"

"Oh, you mean little bitch boy? When we put him in his place?" said Holly, laughing. "That's nothing compared to what I have in mind for the Millennium. If you can't handle that, then I recommend you stay out."

"What do you mean?" asked Pigeon.

"I mean, it might be time for you to fly away, little bird. Before you get hurt," said Holly.

"Here's the way I see it," said Natsumi. "Either you stick with us, or you go crawling back to the freak show that we rescued you from, books and losers and that ridiculous Skeleton Army."

"Just know that if you take option two, you'll be making powerful enemies," threatened Holly. "Choose wisely."

CHAPTER 8
THUS, ALWAYS, NOTHING

"I need to talk to you about something," said Pigeon, shutting the door behind her.

"Is it about the meeting the other day? I don't know how Cherry keeps getting invited to these things," said Sophie "I'm sorry that you had to witness that".

"No," responded Pigeon, shaking her head. "Most of that meeting was Greek to me anyways. I wanted to ask you more about the machine for ghosts."

"What did you want to know?" asked Sophie.

"Ever since I got this chip read by the Watcher, I've been getting phone calls from someone I know is dead," said Pigeon.

"And my work has you convinced I'll be able to help you with this problem?" Sophie asked.

"It all has something to do with your machine for ghosts... and this new Millennium. It all seems to relate," said Pigeon.

Sophie leaned back in her chair and steeped her fingers. "I might have a job for you that can offer some insight." Pigeon nodded, and Sophie proceeded.

"A few months ago, one of my research students absconded with some valuable information. Any attempt to contact or locate this person has been ineffectual. If there is an interrelation between my research and the Millennium Project, this may be the lead you're looking for. Find him, and recover that research."

"So you agree that there is some sort of connection?" asked Pigeon.

Sophie gave the closest thing that a synthetic human could give to a thoughtful silence, and then said, "I think there may be a possibility, perhaps. The logical frame work doesn't exist, but the chance of a correlation is strong."

"What makes you think that?" asked Pigeon.

"You said that everyone is trying to stake a claim on the Millennium, and if I'm being frank, so am I. This missing research is setting back my plans, and your communication with the Watcher seems to be the only loose end," answered Sophie.

"And what is your plan for the Millennium?" asked Pigeon.

"What else have you heard?" asked Sophie.

"I've heard a lot of things," responded Pigeon. "Something about Y2K. Something about how, at midnight, it will leave the City up for grabs."

"If I'm continuing to be frank with you," began Sophie, "my plans do involve the Y2K bug. At midnight on the New Year, I want to see my fellow synthetic humans rise up with their authentic comrades and seize the System for ourselves."

"And then you put microchips in everyone's heads?" asked Pigeon.

"The assimilation process will be swift

and complete, yes. We will boost logical reasoning and efficiency, while doing away with the individual identities that have caused so much conflict and strife. We will create a eutopia, free from sickness and poverty and disease. Where everyone works, and no one starves."

"Sounds like a pipedream," said Pigeon.

"No," responded Sophie. "This is very much a potentiality. If," she added, "you can find me my missing research."

****

When Pigeon arrived in the Green Room, there were several people sitting around the couches, reading. Someone in the corner was watching SYSLink with the volume down low. No one seemed to know where Elizabeth was, until she emerged from the back rooms, yawning.

"Good evening," she said. "Sorry, I was just napping. How are things?"

"Things go," responded Pigeon. "Listen, I need to know: have you referred anyone else to the Watcher lately?" She produced a graduation photo that Sophie had given her.

Elizabeth took the photo, examining it while frowning.

"Yeah, I remember this guy coming through here. You should know you're not the only person looking for him. A Detective Pendleton came through here not long ago with this same photo. I told him to frag off. What's going on?"

"Do you remember what the Watcher told me?" asked Pigeon. Elizabeth nodded. "I've been talking to Sophie, and she said that this man has something to do with the machine for ghosts."

"You've been speaking to Sophie, have you?" asked Elizabeth. "You should be careful around that one. Remember what I told you, about knowledge being power?"

"Yes, why?" asked Pigeon.

"Sophie is knowledgeable, yes. But there is some spark of humanity that her world-view has led her to deny. If Kim follows her heart too much, then Sophie's philosophy has no heart at all."

Pigeon relayed the conversations that she had with Holly, Natsumi, and Sophie while lines of concern etched their way deeper into Elizabeth's face. When Pigeon was done, she nodded thoughtfully then said, "This is worse than I thought. While you're tracking down this missing researcher, I'll need to get in touch with Kim and Lynne. The show of force that we discussed at the last meeting is suddenly the most important thing that we can do."

"Elizabeth! You need to see this!" exclaimed the person watching the TV. Turning up the volume, the whole room watched transfixed as the newscaster reported on the latest of a series of coordinated arrests sweeping the country. A voice over described the ferocity of the crackdown and the intricate inter-agency coordination that made it possible, while images flashed on the screen of Iconoclasts being rounded up and led away. Some chose to fight to the last, but they were quickly put down.

"Hey!" exclaimed Pigeon excitedly, recognising the aesthetic of Holly's followers. "That's the group that Alastair was tracking!"

"This is bad," said Elizabeth, frowning deeper than Pigeon had ever seen her.

"How so?" asked Pigeon. She couldn't help feeling glad to be rid of Holly and her callous brutality.

Elizabeth went to the bookshelf and began running her fingers along the spines, flipping through pages until she produced the information that she was looking for. She handed to book to Pigeon, who saw that it was a book about the history of fascism.

"In his book, Anatomy of Fascism," began Elizabeth, "Paxton found nine mobilizing passions of fascist groups, the common threads that underlie all fascist movements. We know that fascists have always taken power through legitimate means. We also know that, historically, the System has never taken fascist movements seriously until it's too late"

"Okay, so what?"

"If," said Elizabeth, choosing her words deliberately, "the System is rounding up Iconoclasts, it means that their bid for legitimate power has been thwarted. I suspect that they were attempting to usurp the mob in order to secure a place in the System. And, if the System sees the Iconoclasts as a threat, then this may be the existential threat that they need to mobilise towards violence."

"As a fascist group," continued Elizabeth, "they see strength through Darwinian struggle as being above the rule of law. They see themselves as victims, and use that victimhood to justify violence. If they feel that they have been victimised by these arrests, which they almost certainly do, then they are almost certainly preparing for violence as we speak."

"But, aren't most of them in jail now?" asked Pigeon.

"You believe what you see on SYSLink?" scoffed Elizabeth. "And besides, it has never taken a lot of fascists to make a fascism. Mussolini and Hitler both seized power with tiny minorities of supporters. Never underestimate the power of organised hatred."

"So what are you going to do?" asked Pigeon.

"I'll need to get things prepared for this march," responded Elizabeth.

"A march?" It was Pigeon's turn to scoff. "What good will a march be, as a counter to the Iconoclasts? If they are as dangerous as you say they are?"

"Fascism thrives on inaction from the left," responded Elizabeth. "A march is a non-violent show of force. It will show the Iconoclasts that they aren't welcome in Vancouver. It will remind them that we are still here, that we are watching them, and that we are ready to fight, if need be. Lynne is right too: it reaffirms the anti-capitalist, anti-oppressive values that we stand for. It brings unity to our communities, and it shows the System that we won't lie down and allow ourselves to be stamped on."

"So what should I do?" asked Pigeon.

"You go ahead on your own. Once you've found what you need, come back here and we'll go over it together."

"Just like old times," nodded Pigeon.

"Just like them," agreed Elizabeth.

****

Holly stood in the wings of a hand built stage. The band was playing the final song of their set, and the energy in the abandoned factory had reached a fever pitch.

After the last note had rung out, the lights dimmed and she took the centre spotlight. A hush filled the ersatz auditorium. Holly stood, ramrod straight, steadily ratcheting up the tension. When she thought that her audience could take no more, she began to speak. Haltingly at first, but slowly allowing herself to gain momentum, until she was nearly shouting at the top of her lungs:

"I am an apex predator. That means that I can take what I want from whoever I want whenever I want. Being able to do something is the moral justification for doing it. If someone wants to take from me, they must be able to take it. If I can stop them, they have no right to take from me. If someone wants to stop me, they must stop me.

"If they can't stop me, I have a right to take what I want. If I want to take their life, and they don't stop me from taking their life, and I take it, their inability to stop me taking their life gives me the right to take it."

She paused for effect, before continuing, her tone shifting. There was something electric in the air, and she fed off of it, vampiric.

"My daddy once told me that there are only two types of people in the world: creators, and parasites! He me told that creators create and parasites destroy, that creators give to the world while parasites leech from others. I think that he wanted for me to be a creator."

"I chose to be a parasite! Creators are soft, fat, and docile. Parasites do not have that luxury! Creators must, at all times, remain bound to the will and wishes of other creators. Parasites must, at all times, be ready to bring retribution upon all others!"

"Creators give up their freedom in submission to dogmatic hypocrisy! Parasites are truly free and totally uninhibited! Creators must build for themselves or go without! Parasites take as they want!"

"Natural selection! Survival of the fittest! Sic semper nihilim!"

Heart pounding, she saluted her troops, and had the phrase and salute returned.

This is it, she thought. There is no going back.

****

Pigeon was back in the Green Room. When she had attempted to go past the Watcher's place, she had found that it was surrounded by police officers, the entire block cordoned off. Cursing her luck, Pigeon had turned back onto the freeway. This was the only lead she had, and it had been severed all too quickly. Thoroughly dejected, she threw herself down on the bed in Elizabeth's spare room.

She ground the palms of her hands into her eyes, willing her brain to make sense of everything that was happening, but it seemed like it was just too much at once to unscramble. It seemed like there was a weight bearing down on her, something overwhelming just over the horizon, smothering her. Her Runner's Sense screamed in alarm, her senses completely shutting down. The next morning, the day of the march, Pigeon was unable to summon the energy to get herself out of bed. She felt drained, utterly lost, and totally miserable.

"Hey," said Elizabeth knocking softly on the door.

"Hey," replied Pigeon flatly. Her blank stare was fixed on the celling, watching patterns form and shift in the stucco.

"I just wanted to thank you for all of your help. I know you took on a lot of risk by giving us the information that you did. And I want you to know that it's enough. You know?" said Elizabeth.

"Thanks," said Pigeon. Even though she gave no indication, she was touched by Elizabeth's statement. She had never been thanked like this before, and she had never realised how much she missed that validation until just now. Pigeon waited until Elizabeth had left and she was sure she was alone before she got out of bed. A note on the kitchen counter offered her the leftovers in the fridge and encouraged her to check out some of the new additions to the Green Room's collection. Pigeon turned the TV on, flipping through the channels until she found the local SYSLink, where the headline story was the march. Almost a half-million people were expected to attend, and it was slated to shut down much of the downtown core for a sizable portion of the day. She left it on for noise in the background while she fixed herself a bowl of rice and beans.

Apparently, Lynne's objection had been taken seriously, and the bulk of the march was made up of people waving banners calling for decolonisation and indigenous sovereignty. The rest of the protestors were waving handmade signs with anti-gentrification slogans emblazoned on them. Marshalling the march was the Skeleton Army, black banners flying high, each one unique. Some had pirate-style skull and crossbones, but more elaborate ones had full-sized skeletons, or coffins and grave roses, along with the name of the chapter.

Some had come from as far away as the Maritimes to join the protest. At the front of the procession were several Elders, beating drums in time to the pace of the march. A few feet behind them, Pigeon thought she could make out Elizabeth's uneven gait. Orbiting the edges of the march like a flock of scavenging birds were Vancouver's finest, desperately waiting for an excuse to rush in and break up the protest.

When she was finished eating, Pigeon started to pace the room, running her fingers along the spines of the books, mouthing their titles. The Green Room was divided by topic, and the sheer amount of information stored here was staggering. Prison abolition, animal liberation, Marxism, militants, media, disability politics, political theory, labour and organising, feminism… Just when Pigeon thought she had seen everything, she stumbled on a back room that housed even more books. Picking up a few zines at random, Pigeon sat down at the table and began flipping through them idly, admiring the hand drawn artwork.

A sudden loud bang gave her a start, and it took a moment for her to realise that it had come from the TV. There was a shift in the reporter's tone, from professional to panicked, as a series of loud bangs emanated from somewhere off screen. There were screams of pain and horror, confusion as a mass of people began pushing back against the rest of the crowd. No one seemed to be in control, and the police saw this as the perfect opportunity to sweep in and start making arrests.

Then, a series of sharp pops, like too-loud firecrackers. More shrieks, more panic, as the crowd surged back into itself in a hopeless frenzy. A space in the ranks opened up, and the view was of several Skeleton Army members sprawled, bloody on the ground, torn limbs hanging brutally from the force of an explosion. And now, young men clad in camouflage were taking pot-shots at cops in the street, in what was now clearly a coordinated attack.

Another loud bang, this one in the distance, and the camera swung wildly before the feed was switched off. Back to the studio, where a talking head informed the audience that the latest explosion had been at the police headquarters.

Pigeon stared agape, transfixed as events unfolded. Explosions and gunfire were now being reported at intuitions throughout the city: the courts, the library, city hall... She had hardly noticed the passage of time, so when the lock on the front door clicked open it nearly gave her a heart attack.

"Oh my god," gasped Elizabeth, throwing herself through the doorway. Pigeon instinctively threw her arms around her in a tight hug. They spent the rest of the day huddling in front of the television, watching SYSLink scroll past. The list of bombings and casualties kept mounting, as more and more Iconoclast cells took up arms in the name of Holly's cause.

Throughout the day they slowly attracted an audience of refugees; people who, like Pigeon, were unsure of what was happening or what to do, and turned to Elizabeth for guidance, who spent all day in the kitchen, occasionally asking someone to step in while she consoled those who had lost loved ones. They huddled under blankets in the dark, discussing in stern tones the causes and implications of the violence. Around 9:00pm, the System declared a media blackout and with that, the talking heads settled into a routine of stale, repetitive bullet points.

Pigeon's phone rang, the sudden splash of light in the dark catching everyone's attention. She checked the call display and saw that it was Natsumi.

"I have to take this, one second," said Pigeon, getting up and stepping outside. The patio was partially covered, and rain hammered the roof. A chill breeze blew through the openings, and she wished that she had brought the blanket with her.

"Hello?" she answered on the last ring.

"Good-evening!" said Natsumi. It sounded like there was a party going on in the background. "How is my star employee doing on this fine wet night?"

"Good," lied Pigeon. "What's the scan?"

"Only the opportunity of a life time! We're busy celebrating, not sure if you can hear. This is exactly the sort of break through we've been hoping for! We have contractors moving in tomorrow to help clean up the damage. Big money to be made: media partnerships, stock buys, forex. You did good kid. The Company is ordering all of its employees to leave the City. Your card will get you through the checkpoints. There's a safe house in Richmond you can use, your card will get you in there too. And stay in touch. I'm going to need you again, very soon."

Pigeon stood alone, taking in the rain. She needed a break from the heady intellectualism of the Green Room. The full moon peered at her through the clouds, a perfect silver orb.

"Take me," she whispered to the night, spreading her arms. "I'm ready."

"No," the moon whispered back to her. "Not yet."

Pigeon had just lit a smoke when a voice called to her from the dark. A figure stepped into the halo of light, and Pigeon recognised his face instantly, though he was a little older than in the photo she had been given: it was Sophie's missing researcher.

"My name is Noah," he said. "And I need

to   speak   to   Elizabeth   immediately."

CHAPTER 9
DEAD IN THE WATER

Pigeon nearly dropped her cigarette in shock.

"You!" she exclaimed. "Everyone is looking for you."

"I know," he replied. "That's why I'm here. I think I was followed."

"We've got company!" shouted a voice from inside.

Drawing her revolver, Pigeon rounded the front of her house, taking cover behind the broken garden wall. Peering over the top, she saw four Iconclasts clamoring out of an oversized pickup truck, each one wielding some sort of assault weapon. Pigeon slid one of the grenades that Holly had given her into the palm of her hand, pulled the pin, waited a few moments, and then lobbed it underhand towards the back of the truck.

It erupted while it was still in the air, shredding the two guys closest to it. They fell to the ground, writing and screaming, clutching at their faces. Pigeon rounded on the remaining two, firing shots blindly over the top of the wall. They returned fire while she was reloading, chips of cinderblock blasting the top of her head. A brief pause, and she poked her head over the top to see them reloading. She stood up, took aim, and squeezed the trigger twice. The rounds went wide, embedding themselves in the hood of the car.

She quickly ducked back into cover as another hail of gunfire hammered her position. Now, they were alternating, covering each other while the other reloaded so that she was unable to leave her position. Huddled under cover as bullets rained around her, Pigeon swore to herself, digging another grenade out of her pocket. Creeping to the edge of the garden wall, she waited until one of the men shouted "Reloading!" before blindly throwing the grenade, based on where she remembered them to be standing; another explosion and another howl of pain, debris from the ruptured driveway sprinkling her hair.

Suddenly there was a man on top of her, grappling her, an arm around her neck, hand scrabbling at the gun in her hand. Pigeon fired a quick elbow behind her. It connected hard, but he held on, spinning her around and delivering a quick head-butt. Stars popped in front of her eyes, a dull ringing in her ears. She fell to her knees and he kicked her in the chest, sending her sprawling onto her back, gun falling with a thud to the ground. He straddled her chest, pulling his hand back to deliver a knock-out punch. A gunshot, and he fell onto his back screaming and writhing. Scrambling to her feet, Pigeon saw Kim standing over her, a snub nosed revolver held in her outstretched hand.

"Kim!" exclaimed Pigeon.

"In the meat," she said breathlessly. "Now, let's tab out before more of them come."

****

Natsumi lay on her bed, spread-eagle. She was naked, and her synthskin body glistened in the candlelight. She was patched in to the Company feed, and she listened to the combat chatter intently as her lover went down her. He was a meathack, some vat grown and surgically perfected hunk of magazine-cover perfection. Her plastic hair cascaded down the pillow as she dug her fingers into the thick, down comforter. Now he was inside of her, meat against silicone, synthetic nerve endings feeding pleasure to her brain. She wasn't sure which she enjoyed more: the physical sensation, or the knowledge that her account balance was swelling with each passing moment. No, that was a lie. She knew exactly which one she preferred.

****

Neon 2-2, Neon 2-1 over.

2-1, 2-2. Go ahead. Over.

We have enemy foot mobiles at our 3 o'clock. Request suppressing fire. Over.

2-1 copies. Engaging. Out.

****

Krypton 2-6, this is Argon 2-6 Actual. Over.

Argon 2-6 Actual this is Krypton 2-6.

Send it. Over.

We have secured checkpoint X-Ray. Break. Request you retrograde to checkpoint Yankee. We're gonna secure the roadway that runs parallel to checkpoint Yankee, push east to checkpoint Zulu. How copy? Over.

Krypton copies all. We're Oscar Mike in one. Out.

****

Helium FAC, this is Radon. Over.

Radon, this is Helium FAC. We read you loud and clear. Over.

Have eyes on enemy technicals at map grid Delta November 2184175. Hostiles moving south along route Lima. Request fire support. Over.

Radon, you have AC-130 gunship support inbound, callsign Reaper. Standby. Over.

Standing by. Out.

****

Neon 2-2, this is Neon 3-1!

2-2, go ahead.

We are pinned down by enemy foot mobiles with RPGs!

Roger. Can you link up with 3-2?

Negative, we have hostiles approaching at our six! Requesting fire support! Over!

****

Hitman, this is Helium FAC. We have friendlies pinned down by enemy fire at map grid Charlie Uniform 241596. Requesting CAS. Over.

Helium, Hitman. Solid copy. We are inbound, CAS TOT five mikes. Out.

****

Helium, this is Terminator. Over.

Terminator, Helium. Go ahead. Over.

We have eyes on enemy foot mobiles moving south at map grid Alpha Charlie 245417. Request permission to engage. Over.

Roger. Negative on engagement. ROE restricts combat operations near high-value residential areas. Maintain safe distance, and continue to report on enemy disposition. Out.

****

Helium, this is Neon 2-6. Relay for Hitman: BDA is 100/100. Good effect on target, hostiles suppressed. End of mission. Out.

Neon 2-6, Helium. Roger on relay. Out.

****

They were holed up in her Richmond safehouse, huddled in the cold and dark as rain hammered the over –large windows, listening to fighter jets roar and circle and streak overhead. In the distance, they could see bursts of brilliant light: air strikes against the horizon. Unlike in the Green Room, where they had continued to talk politics, they now sat in silence. For Pigeon, there was simply too much to process, let alone converse about, and it seemed as if the sentiment was shared with her new compatriots.

Noah, who had remained speechless despite his assertion that he needed to speak to Elizabeth, was the first to break the silence.

"We need to go back."

"No way," said Kim, shaking her head.

"My research isn't complete, but it might offer us a way to stop all of this," he responded.

"What is your research?" asked Elizabeth, genuinely curious.

"I am building wetware/software interfaces," he responded simply. Elizabeth frowned. Evidently she knew what he was talking about, and didn't like it.

"And how will that put an end to the violence?"

"In order to bypass the System, I've had to use an atypical interface. It should allow me to perform a server reboot, inject malicious code all throughout the System," he gestured with his hands, implying a large explosion.

"No way," repeated Kim. "After all the shit we had to pull just to get out of the City, and that was before it turned to an active war zone. She shook her head again. "No way."

"I'll do it," said Pigeon, speaking up, Anita's ghostly phone call still fresh in her mind. She went to the spare bedroom and pulled a panel away from the wall, revealing a small arms cache. "Let's get this done."

Pigeon spread Kim's map of the city out on the coffee table, weighing down the edges with machine pistols she had retrieved from the other room

"We need to get from here," she pointed out their location on the map, "to here," she indicated the location the Noah had given her. "We know that they have checkpoints here, here, and here. Which means that we need to find a way into the city that doesn't cross one of those main bridges."

"Sounds impossible," said Kim.

"Not if we use the network of old rail tunnels running underneath the city. There should be one here, that will take us under the Fraser River and drop us a few blocks from where we need to be."

"Who else knows about these tunnels?" asked Elizabeth knowingly.

"Well, that's the bad news," said Pigeon, scratching her head. "Even without the System breathing down our necks, we can still expect to have to watch our backs."

"I've never used a gun before," said

Noah, raising his hand.

"Then you'd better stick close to me," responded Pigeon. "Who else is in?" Hesitantly, Kim and Elizabeth agreed.

****

Bouncing over the rotted railroad ties, Pigeon flicked on the high beams. She slowed to a crawl, her mind playing tricks on her, every tattered shadow an Iconoclast.

"Is this what it's like to Run?" asked Kim.

"No," responded Pigeon. "Running is solo, trying to stay cold, distant, uninvolved. This is the opposite of Running. I'm done Running. This ends tonight."

Pulling out onto the street on the other side, Pigeon killed the lights entirely. The last thing they needed to do was announce their presence to the world. In the distance, they could hear the pops and clatters of machine-gun fire, interjected with the roar of echoing explosions. Fighter jets streaked overhead, and her Runner's Sense fed her images of them dropping their deadly payload at any moment, landing directly on top of them, annihilating them. Fortunately though, no such thing happened. In fact, they encountered no resistance whatsoever, the fighting seeming to be concentrated in the eastern part of the City. Near Holly's compound, she realised.

The laboratory was cold, poorly lit, books laying open on tables like dead butterflies. In the centre of the room was a large mainframe, all whirring fans and blinking lights, exposed cables ran crisscrossed along the floor, snaking into wall sockets. One wall was caved in, wiring spilling onto the floor and finding its way into the machine. A bedroll lay in the corner, next to an unfinished bowl of cheap ramen noodles.

"We need to jack in," said Noah. Elizabeth and Kim dutifully lay down on the ground and began rolling up their sleeves, but Pigeon hesitated.

"Quickly, we don't have much time," urged Noah. Laying down next to the others and bracing herself, she feed the input jack into the relay on her forearm.

Blinking in the sudden sunlight, Pigeon fought to gain her bearings. The simulation pulled at the edges of her consciousness, pushing her further into the shared dream. Elizabeth, Kim and Noah stood in a semi-circle around her, each wearing the same, identical white terrycloth robe. The space was white, not blank, but clean. The smell of fresh laundry hung in the air. Sunlight shone brilliantly through large bay windows, reflecting off of ocean waters. In the distance, Pigeon could hear the pounding of the surf.

"This way," said Noah, leading them through an ornate set of double-doors. Up a set of equally ornate marble stairs, and they were in what appeared to be some sort of hotel. Guests in matching robes greeted Noah formally, and he returned the greeting: flats, 2D sprite renderings of living people, intended to round out the population of the place, make it seem less empty than it really was. As they approached the front desk, Pigeon began to feel sick. She hated cyberspace, but this was something else. Something dark, unbidden, rose in her mind. She was being followed. Whipping around, she saw no one.

"Who else is in this simulation?" she asked Noah under her breath.

"Just us", he said, then turned to the concierge.

"Good afternoon, Shelley. I'll be needing to close down the sim," he said briskly.

"Going somewhere?"

Pigeon looked around for the source of the voice, but no one else seemed to have reacted. Elizabeth was engrossed in the folds of her robe, rubbing the material thoughtfully, while Kim stood at the window, watching the simulated surf crash against rocks made from ones and zeroes. Noah was deep in conversation with Shelley, some technobabble that she didn't understand. Finally he emerged from the conversation, a frown etching itself into his smooth simfeatures.

"The wetware isn't interfacing," he said simply.

"So we're dead in the water, then?" asked Elizabeth.

"It says it wants to speak to Pigeon," he replied suspiciously. All three of them turned to face Pigeon, her face flushing.

Noah led them too an elevator, that took them to the top floor, a roof top garden. No, not a garden, but a park. Pigeon recognised it almost immediately. It was the park where she had met Anita. As the four dreamers approached the centre of the park, the dream began to feel more like a memory, though

Pigeon began to notice certain things out of place. An oriental garden where there hadn't been one, trees of the wrong species, weeping willows instead of battered old oaks. A water feature, something the City certainly never would have paid for. But aside from that, exactly how she had remembered it. Even the sun beating down on them, though now it was tempered by a cool sea breeze. In the distance, she could hear the sound of the surf pounding.

Steering the party away from the centre of the park, she led them towards the spot where they had sat that whole summer, finding instead a pagoda. It was cast in ominous shadows that seemed to emanate from the structure itself. Pigeon shivered.

"Say what you need to, but make it quick," instructed Noah, as the others hung back with him.

Grimacing, Pigeon stepped into the pagoda. As she did so, the dream shifted. She was sixteen again, in the CHEEK, walking down a brick corridor, flanked by two flats dressed as security officers. She knew where they were leading her, because she had been there before: the isolation cells, deep in the bowls of the complex. Cell number 9. It had been her only home for months, the punishment for her inequities.

She passed through the door way and the dream shifted again. She found herself in a space that was darker than dark and colder than cold, and for a moment, Pigeon was terrified that she had brain-died. But no, there was a life here, some thrumming in the dark. She reached out with her mind until she could feel herself make contact with the source. There was a brief squall in her ears, like an old internet connection attempting to find a server, and then silence.

"Hello?" she said hesitantly.

"Hello, babe," said Anita. "You've finally come."

Pain.

More pain than she had ever thought possible, coursing from her brain throughout her entire body. Spots popped in front of her eyes and she willed herself not to lose consciousness. Then, the world went dark.

A blinding flash of light and a searing pain her frontal lobe, and Pigeon was awake again, rolling onto her side just in time to throw up. Memories cascaded through her brain, thoughts that weren't hers. Images, memories which belonged to someone else, a childhood that was never hers. Meeting herself, seeing a lonely teenager sitting alone on a park bench. Flatlining alone in a tenement, while her girlfriend visits violence on a rival dealer. Dying real brain-death, and then darkness, new life, reborn as something unnatural.

Voices, shouting:

"What have you done?"

"You've ruined everything."

"She always ruins everything."

"She's worthless."

"She's useless."

She dry heaved, rolled away from the puddle of vomit and scrambled to her feet. They were standing on a beach, the hotel before them aflame, a single point of light in a day that had become unexpectedly dark and stormy. She crawled to her feet, wincing in pain and clutching at her skull. It felt like someone had put red-hot railway spikes into her eyeballs.

"It's just you and me now, babe," said Anita's disembodied voice.

"What's going on?" asked Pigeon.

"The time has come for you to choose."

"Choose what?"

"Remember what I said, about our lives moving like clockwork? Like we are being drawn forward by destiny?"

"Yes."

"Well, this is it, babe. The end of the line. The clock is striking midnight."

"What should I do?"

"I don't know, what should we do?"

"Noah said that his research- this simulation, this thing…"

"Me, what I've become."

"I am so sorry baby. I don't know what's happening anymore. Nothing makes sense."

"Think. I can see your memories, fragments of them anyways. I know that you have all the information you need."

"Noah said that we could take down the System." Pigeon sighed and ran her hands over her head. Pain pulsed in time to her heartbeat. "But if we do, there are people waiting in the wings to pick up the pieces."

"What people?" urged Anita. "What do they want?"

"Holly and the Iconoclasts… they want violence, to sort out the weak from the strong. Natsumi and the Company want to build the Millennium Project, turn the city into a resort town for the super-rich. Sophie and Noah, they want more of this. Robots and simulations and… and they seem to believe in the greater good but my God, they seem to be willing to go to any length to get there."

"Utopia at any cost?"

"Exactly."

"Are those the only options?"

"Well, there is also Elizabeth and the Green Room. She believes in building a world without any sort of System, utopian or otherwise. She wants people to stand on their own, to help each other and build communities."

"That sounds edgy. How do we make it happen?"

"I don't... I don't know. That's the problem. We can't just give her this power, because I don't think it's something that you can make happen, and I think that's the point. It's something that people need to choose. I'm afraid that if we abolish the System, that someone else will step in to will the vacuum. But I don't know what else to do."

"So we break down the System, and we hope for the best?"

"I guess so," sighed Pigeon. "I hate that it's so hard to know what the right thing to do is, but I can't imagine what else we can do."

"Then let's do it, and hope for the best."

"God, I hope this works."

"Me too, babe."

"I love you."

"I love you, so mu-"

The pain again, forcing her to shudder violently, shaking her from the dream, gasping for breath. She came too, drifting in and out of consciousness. She heard shouting, words that didn't make sense. She rolled over on her side. Detective Pendleton, waving a side arm, flanked by two Kuroyama mercenaries, desperately trying to restore order. Holly, with an assault rifle dangling from her finger tips, pacing like a caged animal. Noah in between them, speaking softly, like a mother to an unruly child. She couldn't see Kim or Elizabeth.

"He's a murderer!"

"I never killed anyone!"

"Oh, so a grave robber, then. Really upstanding!"

"All in the name of progress, right?"

Pigeon rolled on to her other side; there was a machine pistol laying on the ground, just out of her reach.

"Play time is over. Now, hand me the chip. The time for retribution is upon us."

"The chip won't do you any good. It's already been downloaded and wiped."

"Bullshit. I want what's mine."

Pigeon inched her fingers closer to the

firearm, nails scrabbling against the cold concrete.

"Will someone please explain to me just what the hell is going on?"

"The only person who can do that, officer, is unconscious right now."

"All we need is her brain, dead or alive. Isn't that right, Noah? You've resurrected the dead before, no reason you can't do it again."

"Like hell," whispered Pigeon. Her fingers finally closing over the muzzle of the machine pistol, she flipped it around in her hand and pressed it against her temple.

"Oh, hell no! Put the gun down right this second!"

"That's not going to happen, officer."

"You're in over your head here."

Pigeon began to laugh involuntarily, the absurdity of the situation overwhelming. A moment passed, where time seemed to dilate. Pigeon could feel her heart beat in her throat. Once, twice. The tension in the air was palpable.

Now! screamed her Runner's Sense.

With an animal howl, Pigeon sent a spray of bullets in the direction of the Kuroyama mercenaries as the room erupted in thunder. Sparks and debris filled the air, bullets ricocheting off of every surface, the mainframe in the centre of the room sparking and stuttering as it tore apart. Someone had Pigeon by the feet, was dragging her into cover.

"Covering fire!"

A burst of spent casings fell all around her, a deadly downpour.

"We need to move now!"

"I'm pinned down!"

Pigeon was still fading in and out as she was half-carried down a flight of dirty stairs, and then dumped unceremoniously in a heap.

"Stay here," instructed Holly.

The sound of an explosion, screams of pain. Gunfire. The low, pulsating roar of a helicopter, hovering overhead. Pigeon struggled to her feet, tried to get her bearings, then collapsed again. A dull pain thundered in her temples, building in intensity until the world started to fade into a grey blur. She gasped for breath, willing herself not to lose consciousness, but teetering on the brink.

More gunfire now, quickly petering out as one side gained the upper hand. Suddenly, there was a form leering over her. She drew her side arm, pulled the trigger, but the hammer struck an empty chamber. A fist came down on her, hard, and she lost the loose grip on consciousness that she had been struggling to maintain. A brief image flashed through Pigeon's mind, her and Anita hugging in the park, and then the world went black once again.

****

When Pigeon came too, the first thing she saw was white. Cyberspace? No, this wasn't a dream. The CHEEK? Too clean. The smell of bleach was in the air. She rolled over in bed, and saw that she was wearing mint green scrubs. A hospital. Rain lashed the single small window. In the distance, sirens wailed. From the hallway, the hustle and bustle of medical professionals tending to their patients. The ceiling lights were dimmed, and Pigeon cast her eyes around in the gloom, trying desperately to plan a Run.

From what she could see through the

window, she was several stories up. So that was a no-go. Air vent maybe? Or would she have to go through the main door? The thought of taking hostages flitted across her mind. A scalpel, syringe, anything she could use as a weapon. Nothing.

She tried to stand up, but she was handcuffed to the bed, restraints at her writs and ankles. Trapped. Finally, he slumped back into bed, defeated.

"Oh, you're awake! My name is Lindsey, I'll be your nurse today. The doctor will be by later, we weren't sure when you'd come around. In the meantime, we have a visitor."

"Mom?"

"No, a business associate. Should I let her in?"

Pigeon nodded, yes. Her neck cracked, stiff from resting at an awkward angle. There was a dull pounding in her head, a lingering pain. She was hoping it would be Kim or Elizabeth.

"What's the scan?" she asked dully, as Natsumi closed the door behind her.

"You must think you're a real hero."

"Not at all. I just took the choices that were offered to me."

"You dealt a mortal blow to the System. I just wanted you to know that."

"So what does that mean?"

"There's an election next year. The Party is expected to lose. Records on all the Runners have been erased. People's faith has been shaken, and they're turning to the private sector to deliver answers."

"Sounds like you've won."

"I always win. I told you, I am deus ex machina, and god doesn't play dice with the universe. Noah and Sophie were brought in for conspiracy to commit treason. Holly is missing, presumed dead. It's just you and me, kiddo."

"Kim, Elizabeth?"

"They've skipped town. The Skeleton Army is mostly broken up, either dead or in jail. Holly got to the Green Room, torched it to the ground."

"Jesus. And the Y2K?"

"The Company will make a pretty penny

off of software upgrades, but it should pass without much incident, thanks to you. Of course, the Millenium Project is still slated to meet its targets by 2009. But overall, I should give you a big damn bravo."

"So what do you want from me?"

"Nothing. Consider your contract terminated. I pulled some strings, and your criminal charges will be served here, under constant medical supervision. My parting gift from me to you. I owe you one."

Rain hammered the small window, dark clouds shifting in the wind. She wasn't dead, and she wasn't going to face the consequences of her actions. The two key components of a successful Run. Maybe this was sign. That she didn't need to Run anymore. Pigeon heaved a deep sigh, and tried to get comfortable. She was ready for the long haul.

After all, she remembered, the sun always comes out.

Eventually.

Manufactured by Amazon.ca
Acheson, AB